You, Me & Mr. Blue Sky

Elisa Lorello & Craig Lancaster

LANCARELLO
ENTERPRISES

Text copyright © 2019 by Elisa Lorello and Craig Lancaster
All rights reserved

Printed in the United States of America.

Published by Lancarello Enterprises, 1219 Frost Street, Billings, MT 59105

ISBN-10: 0-9976433-3-1
ISBN-13: 978-0-9976433-3-6

For Jane Estelle. We miss you.

Jo-Jo

In a world of beginnings, I'm at the end

GREAT. New Year's Eve. Twenty-eighteen staring me right in the face, telling me to step in and make myself at home. The people around me shaking the dust and the rust off twenty-seventeen and getting ready for renewal. If they've had a bad year, they hope for something more glorious from the coming one. If they've had a good year, they hope for a continuation of their fortune. Tomorrow, every intention will be pure, every wish will be for peace and prosperity, and every possibility will be alive. Refreshing, isn't it?

No. Not particularly.

You know what I'm going to do tomorrow? I'm going to write a group e-mail, the kind where you put your own address in the "to:" field and everybody else in "bcc:" because you don't want anyone else to know who's seeing it. In it, I'll tell everybody I care about, and everybody who cares about me, that the calendar is now clear on March 1st, that Rex and I won't be getting married on the banks of the Yellowstone River after all, that Rex and I won't be getting married anywhere ever, in fact, and that I'm terribly sorry to deliver this bad news. I'll tell them all that I'm OK—no, no, that I'm *fine*, and that everything happens for the best, and that my biggest days and the most wonderful realizations of my dreams are yet to come. All of which is probably a lie.

And then I'll hit "send" and I'll stare at my computer screen and wait for the responses to come in. The ones from people who will use words to say they have no words. The ones from people who will ask me if I need anything (yes, but it's nothing I'll ever have). The ones from people who will tell me they're heartbroken. (And I will resist the urge to say, "Oh, no, you don't know what heartbroken is.") The ones from people who will say, "You know, Jo-Jo, I always suspected Rex was no good." They'll say this even though they've indicated nothing of the sort before. Never mind that it's true. Why didn't they say it then? What kind of friend says such a thing now? I don't know. But I'll find out tomorrow.

The ones I'm dreading most will be from people who will tell me they know how I feel. Those will hurt. Because, no, you don't know how I feel. You don't have a clue, and I don't have the motivation to explain it to you. And that's why I will tell you this news by e-mail rather than face to face. Because if you say that directly to me, I will punch you in the throat.

I'll sit at my computer, and I'll read every response, and I'll write back with two little words: "Thank you." I will answer no questions. I will swallow every urge to write back and argue or defend myself— or, God help me, defend Rex, who has a dog's name but none of a dog's charm. I will resist those impulses because these people love me, and because I love them.

Of course, Rex said he loved me, too, and look how that turned out.

HERE'S THE THING THAT REALLY MAKES ME ANGRY, now that I've had a few hours to consider it: I almost begged Rex not to go because it's New Year's Eve and we're supposed to be at Larry and Jennifer's party tonight, and how cruel is it to break up with somebody on a holiday? I almost *begged*. As if it's not a huge relief that he figured out he can't do this now, rather than a day or two before the wedding. As if I would want still want him after something so pathetic as "Jo-Jo, here's the thing: I'm just not ready. I'm not ready to settle down and commit myself to a town and a house and a person till death do us part." Perhaps you've noticed, as I did, that I was number three in his list of non-commitments. Perhaps you'll notice, as I did, that he's a forty-three-year-old man, too far into his life to be discovering himself and thus a long shot to figure out in another year, or five or ten more of them, that he really *can* commit to a town or a house or a person.

Or me. And I'm thirty-nine.

And then he said the part that almost got me. He said, "It's not that I don't love you."

That's when I almost begged. I said "please," and then what was coming up behind that word got caught in my filter long enough for me to realize something: he couldn't say he loved me without a double negative. Immediately, I adjusted course.

So it came out like this: "Please. Fine. Leave now."

"Huh?"

"Leave now."

And he did. One suitcase, one duffel bag, one pat on Cholly's head, and Rex was gone.

He must be so relieved.

So I'm going to Larry and Jennifer's. Alone. As I should be. As I'm going to be from now on. And it's going to be fine.

Fine.

Linus

All I did was wonder how your arms would be ...

I'M GOING TO COME RIGHT OUT AND SAY IT: being alone sucks. Anyone who tells you that you're somehow less of a person because you prefer to be in a relationship has either (a) thrown in the towel, or (b) gulped the Oprah Kool-Aid. My therapist and I used to argue about this from time to time, and she didn't convince me otherwise.

It's not that I disrespect people who prefer to be single. I just don't understand it. Like, I literally don't get it. As if it were a foreign language or an alien culture.

Last December thirty-first, I gave myself a year to get over my divorce. Didn't date, did therapy, took cooking classes, and stayed off social media. Amanda got remarried. To Bryce, our (now her) accountant. Whom she slept with while we were still married. That was difficult, but at this point I wish her no ill will. She's happy now. That's what matters. Our divorce was as amicable as a divorce can be despite the betrayals. Eventually, I realized I didn't want her if she didn't want me, but I still wish her happiness, you know? Still, just because a divorce is amicable doesn't mean it isn't a shitshow. It's only now that I can see how miserable Amanda was—never mind how miserable I was, because I already knew that—and how we're better off apart. But at the time of the unraveling, I didn't want us to be apart. I clung to togetherness for dear life. I've learned a few things since then.

Anyway ...

I'm OK. I'm forty-one and healthy. I've got Toby, the two-year-old tuxedo cat I rescued from a shelter after I moved out and bought a fixer-upper on the south side of Billings. My business is breathing on its own, albeit a bit fledgling, my football team will be in the playoffs, and I'm ready. Like, totally ready.

For Jennifer and Larry's party, that is. But ready to start dating, too.

In fact, that's my New Year's Resolution. Or rather, my New Year's Intention. Resolutions are overdone, and mostly destined to fail. Intentions seem more noble. Both connote things you will do, soon, in the near future, sometime. But my therapist told me that intentions are more immediate. They go out into the universe the moment they're uttered or incanted or declared or announced, and the universe or God or the Flying Spaghetti Monster starts lining things up for you. Less vending machine and more project management, I guess. So, yeah, my intention is to be in a relationship again. Because I'll cop to this: I *liked* being married. I liked the routine and the partnership. I liked the companionship, the reliability on one another, the give and take, the conversations, and, you know, the love and stuff.

The fact that I didn't want to be married to Amanda anymore was Amanda-and-me-specific, not reflective of my general attitude about relationships. People should pair off, I think. *I* should pair off.

Problem was that I got complacent when I was married to Amanda. And hence she got bored, and ... well, let's not go back there. We've both moved on, with lessons learned. I wish her all the best. Have I said that? Well, I do.

This time, my intention isn't just to be in a relationship, but to get it right. Go long with the big L. Fall in love, cherish her, be kind, be more giving in that give and take, and most of all, be *attentive* this time.

JENNIFER AND LARRY KIND OF ADOPTED ME THIS PAST YEAR. Dinner at their house once a week, and Jenn usually sent me home with a casserole (hence the cooking classes so she'd no longer feel obligated; now we just swap recipes). Invited me to little Charlie's soccer games (I'm officially "Uncle Linus"). Helped me get my contracting business going with word-of-mouth, and were the only ones who didn't chastise me for quitting the predictability and security of my teaching job for something that's more of a high-wire act. I owe them, big time. No idea how I'll ever repay them—a gift card ain't gonna cut it. But hopefully I'll be able to do something. Something extraordinary. Like renovating their kitchen. I don't mean to say it's a bad kitchen. I just mean they deserve a kitchen that puts all other kitchens to shame. And I'm the guy who can give them that.

To be honest, I felt like staying home tonight and switching back and forth between every series marathon on TV. But again, Jennifer and Larry. How could I say no? And they'd have thought I was sulking or something. So I went, and I wore the blue-striped button-down shirt my mother gave me for Christmas this year. (She gives me two button-down shirts every year—one for Christmas and one for my birthday, both from the Gap.) She says I look good in blue, that it brings out my eyes. Amanda used to say the same thing. Then again, Amanda's been blind as a bat since the third grade. Metaphorically speaking, that is. No offense to blind people. Or bats.

Of course, once I got to the party, my anti-social inklings from earlier dissipated. The alcohol may have had something to do with that.

Jennifer made everyone write down a New Year's Resolution on a non-sticky sticky note, sign our name, and place it in a jar marked TO BE OPENED 12-31-18 AT 11:45 P.M. in a thick Sharpie and underlined three times. "Be serious, people," she said. "No stupid shit." The point is to open the jar this time next year, read the resolutions out loud, and see which ones got fulfilled. So I did it. I scribbled: *Fall completely, unequivocally, deliciously in love and be in a committed relationship. Linus Travers, 12-31-17 10:32 p.m.* And into the jar it went, mixing in with the other colorful folded squares. Looked like confetti. Or rainbow-colored hail.

I felt buoyant, and not from the booze. No, I saw that jar as a direct connection to ... what? I don't know. Maybe someone who could do something about all those intentions. Like the fictional stork delivering babies to eagerly waiting parents. Only this wasn't fiction.

But, geez, I didn't see it coming.

I hadn't really noticed her mingling. Never even got her name. It's not that she blended into the furniture. She had on this red dress with a beaded necklace and long black hair, so she was hard to miss, unless you're willfully unobservant. But this is what gets me in trouble all the time. If you want details, I'm your man, but I sometimes miss the big things. Never saw my divorce coming, for example. Sacked me from the back. And in this case, precisely at midnight, after we counted down the final ten seconds and threw streamers and banged on noisemakers and blew into our kazoos, and all the couples paired off and started kissing each other, she just came up to me.

"What's your name?" she asked.

I started to answer, and she said, "Never mind. Doesn't matter."

"OK."

"So, listen, congratulations, whoever you are. I'm gonna kiss you, and then I'm done." She then pulled me by the collar toward her, wrapped her arms around my neck, and planted her lips on mine.

Her full, supple, glossy, delectable lips. She even slipped her tongue in there.

Afterward, in a self-satisfying way, she nodded her head, said, "OK," and walked away. Just like that. Leaving me there, mouth open, with nacho and whisky breath, completely wowed.

Who'd have thought it would happen so soon?

Mr. Blue Sky

This is where I come in

HELL OF A SITUATION WE'VE GOT HERE, HUH? Girl wants nothing to do with love anymore. Boy wants nothing more than to love and be loved. And here they've collided at a nice little gathering in Billings, Montana, of all places. On my watch, as it turns out.

Let me try to explain what that means. I'm what you would probably call a guardian angel, and it just so happens that Jo-Jo and Linus are part of what you might call my "caseload." More on that in a minute.

Here's the thing: This wasn't my doing, at least not in any overt way. I didn't look at Jo-Jo Middlebury and Linus Travers and say, "You know who'd make a good couple? These two. Let it be." The fact is, I know no such thing and have no such power. What's more, the very definition of my work requires me to think unilaterally rather than in a binary way. Put more simply, in my capacity as your guardian angel, I'm all about you and nobody else. Further, I don't get involved in human endeavors in that kind of ham-handed way. If the bus is gunning for you, I might scream *Run!* but I'm not going to give you a push, as much as I may want to. You probably think I should, given my job description and title, but I'm just not hardwired to do it, and anyway that's not the way this thing works. There are laws. I'm also not some kind of game-show host, handing out prizes. (Although there is a kind of a *Let's Make a Deal* thing going on in that you constantly get to make choices. And how you respond to those choices is totally up to you, even if you wind up with a year's worth of canned squid. The silly costumes are optional.) But, hey, I'm getting ahead of myself here …

Let's start again, this time with an introduction. I am … well, that's just it. *I am.* This is the part that always trips everyone up. Explaining it in a language you, a human being, can comprehend is a dicey proposal. In short, it would blow your mind. So let's use your words going forward, eh?

I do have a name, but it isn't anything you would be able to easily pronounce, like *Bob.* More like something tonal, such as whale songs or the signal those aliens in *Close Encounters of the Third Kind* responded to. (Although, seriously—a *tuba*? You've got all those cool Moog synthesizers, John Williams, and you use a *tuba*? What about a tuba says *celestial*?) Humans have some ideas about the hierarchies and structures, but let's just leave it at this: you have no clue. I don't say that to be dismissive. It's just a fact, Jack.

I prefer to set aside the dogma and the philosophy and get down to the atoms, if you will. Have you ever looked at your newborn and had that rush of emotion, the thoughts and feelings competing for space in your head and your heart, where you're suddenly scared for the world this little life is inheriting and buoyant over the possibilities that lie ahead? That's me being with you, quietly counseling you.

I live in the moments between the molecules.

I'm there when you wake up at sunrise, just you, and you marvel at the beauty of the world you live in. I'm sometimes the still, small voice. I'm the last strand of comfort when the wolves are at the door. I'm also the one who can't believe the last good program on television, *Mary Tyler Moore*, ceasted production in 1977. I wasn't done yet, morons.

There's much I could tell you about how I work, but what's the point? It's not going to make a material difference in your life, which is just a whisper of time in the great scheme of things. I don't wish to be rude, but I've seen many of you come and will see many of you go, in the sense of life on earth, and the truth is that your time there is going to blink on and blink off while I'm still rubbing the sleep out of my eyes, cosmically speaking. What I'm really trying to say is that even though I have significant purpose, as do you, yours plays out in a blip, a gleam. So don't get too wound up in me. Instead, go forth and be the best person you can be. Find *your* purpose and live it. I have some thoughts about how you can do that, and interestingly enough, I think Jo-Jo and Linus can help illustrate them, regardless of what happens or doesn't happen from here. So let's see where this goes, eh?

I'll jump in every now and then with a little color commentary— I'm no John Madden, but I have my moments, and more important I have the time. I'll keep the train moving, so to speak. But let me be clear: I don't know what's going to happen any more than you do. There wouldn't be much point in my job if I got to commandeer all the big decisions. Especially since I'm not responsible for giving life in the first place. Think about that. And if you really want to consider the immensity of what I'm talking about, think about this: It makes no difference to me. I don't say that to be callous, but rather to be truthful. In matters of purpose and intention, I am without judgment.

Oh, right. I still haven't introduced myself. Well, because you're more comfortable with names (and because some of you are tone deaf), call me Mr. Blue Sky.

You know, Electric Light Orchestra?

Jeff Lynne?

From the album *Out of the Blue*, released in 1977?

Hey, sit on it, Potsie. The 1970s were a really good decade for me.

While we're setting the record straight, I should note that I'm neither male nor female. Or maybe I'm both. (See what I mean? I'm a mass of contradictions.) I can't bend to the way you understand sex or gender. And I don't have wings. Or a cape. Or telekinetic powers. But I can recite every alphabet in every language—human or otherwise—backward. That takes talent.

But, really, have you ever listened to that song? "Mr. Blue Sky"? It's brilliant.

Now, go away for a while. Mr. Blue Sky needs to scrounge up some lunch.

Linus

Welcome to the first day of the rest of your life

I WOKE UP IN JENNIFER AND LARRY'S GUEST ROOM. I didn't think I'd had *that* much to drink, but Jennifer is—and I say this with all the love in my heart for her—a bit of a mother hen. She took my keys away.

The party wound down around two a.m. The mystery kisser must have left immediately after she planted one on me, because I couldn't find her—and believe me, once I regained my bearings, I looked. I pretty much know every inch of Jennifer and Larry's house, so it wouldn't raise their hackles if I started opening doors and poking my head in places where others would be unwelcome. I looked in the pantry. I looked in Charlie's room. I looked in Jennifer and Larry's en suite. I even skulked around the basement, thinking maybe Mystery Woman had slipped away to smoke a joint or something.

Nowhere.

She sure as hell moved into my head, though. Like, prime real estate.

I padded in my stocking feet into the kitchen, where Jennifer was drinking black coffee and coaxing Charlie to eat his Mini-Wheats. She was makeup-free and wearing sweats, her dyed blonde hair clumsily in a ponytail. Some women are so obviously not blondes, but Jennifer pulled off the look rather well, I thought.

"Ah, look who's here," she said. "Uncle Linus."

I tousled Charlie's red hair (he takes after his dad). "You look like you slept in your clothes," he said.

"I did," I replied. "Your pajamas didn't fit me." He giggled. To Jenn, I said, "Where's your studmuffin?"

She huffed. "Out running," she said.

My face twisted in incredulity. "In this tundra?"

"January first. When people do dumb things in the name of 'resolution.' So, Happy New Year, friend. You have a good time last night?"

"Swell," I replied as she poured a mug of coffee and set it in front of me. "So, listen, there was this woman here last night..." I started, then stopped, wondering if I should proceed in front of the kid. But he was fixated on the back of the cereal box as if he were reading *The New York Times*, and Jenn was looking at me expectantly.

"Who?" she asked.

"That's the thing. I didn't get her name. She had long black hair and was wearing a red dress and beads and—"

"Sounds like Jo-Jo."

Jo-Jo. God, even her name was sexy. Yeah. She was totally a Jo-Jo.

"You know her?" I asked. "I mean, obviously you know her or she wouldn't have been here last night. But—"

Jenn interrupted me again. "Stop right there, sweetie. I don't know what your angle is here, but I see the moony eyes. So let me just tell you: she's engaged. Like, super-engaged. Like, the wedding is exactly two months from today."

She might as well have just kicked me in the stones. *Engaged*? Well, that's that.

Except ...

Why would someone who was "super-engaged" kiss *me*, a total stranger? And what was that she said right before she kissed me? *I'm done.*

Either she needed to sow one more oat or she's done with being engaged. And let's face it: if you're sowing oats before the big M, your relationship is in trouble.

Either way, I wasn't less intrigued.

"I'm just asking," I said. "I didn't see her with anyone last night. And we had a nice exchange, so I thought I'd inquire."

"Larry's a better person to ask," Jenn said. "They go way back. In fact, they were almost a thing."

"What kind of thing?"

"Like, a Mr.-and-Mrs.-Morelli thing."

I did an involuntary spit-take of my coffee, which sent Charlie into convulsive laughter.

"Geezus, Linus," Jenn said as she sprang from her seat while I attempted to wipe the table with my sleeve. She pushed my hand out of the way with a dish towel and mopped the rest of it up.

"How did I not know about this?" I asked.

"It's ancient history," she said. "Long before I knew him, and long before you knew us."

"And you're OK with her being friends with him?"

"Of course. I trust her completely around Larry, and I trust him completely, too," she said, although breaking eye contact with me as she said it. Charlie abandoned the half-empty bowl and us for his PlayStation (in my day it was Atari). I remained slackjawed. "He fully disclosed their relationship to me when we first started dating.

No red flags. They were a thing, and then they became friends after they realized they were better suited to be friends than married. It happens. Kind of mature, if you ask me." She said it all very matter-of-factly.

I pressed again: "How come I never knew this?"

"You don't pay attention."

The comment stung. And she was wrong—it's not that I don't pay attention, it's that I subconsciously pretend I haven't noticed.

"Why are they better off as friends?" I quickly tacked on. "Just curious."

"Again, Larry is a better person to ask. He said she was difficult to know. Not a bad person, just one of those people where the challenge is attractive, until you realize just how challenging she is."

I cogitated on this while Jenn buttered a piece of toast for me. I told you. Mother hen.

"How is *your* relationship with her?" I asked.

"I agree with Larry; she's hard to know. At least that's been my limited experience with her. We don't go out for coffee or anything one-on-one like that, but I like her just fine." Again, Jenn broke eye contact before resuming. "She's smart. Like, whip-smart, not educated. And not to say that she's not educated, just not an academic, know what I mean?"

"What does she do?"

"Opened a gym, I think. She's tough. Like, driven. When she wants what she wants, look out."

I didn't dare say anything to Jenn, but if she was intending to blunt my curiosity, she was doing a terrible job. I turned the name over and over in my head: Jo-Jo. *Hey, ho, Jo-Jo!*

"OK," I said. "Good to know." I ate my toast in three bites.

"But like I said, Linus, she's engaged," Jenn said.

"I know."

"Off-limits."

"I know."

"And even if she wasn't, I'd tell you not to expend your energy. I think she'd eat you up and spit you out, and I'd hate to see that happen, because then I'd have to kill her."

"OK," I said. I stood up. "Um, can I have my keys? Sorry to eat and run, but I gotta feed Toby."

She opened the flour jar and pulled them out, jingling them as she did to shake off the snowy excess.

"Thanks for everything," I said, and I kissed her on the cheek. I called out "later, dude," to Charlie, grabbed my shoes and coat from the guest room, and left through the back door. The moment I settled into in my car, I took out my iPhone and asked Siri to give me a list of gyms within a twenty-mile radius.

Jo-Jo

The best-laid plans, and other stupid stuff

I DID WHAT I SAID I'D DO. And let's be clear: I always do what I say I'm going to do. It's what happens after I do it that can't be controlled, and that simple fact explains so much about what's wrong in my life. *So much.* I can't even get into it now. I have the energy for one task, and that's deciding if I'm going to open my gym—broken promises there, too. Rex is gone. Now it's me, Cholly the wonder Lab, and a handful of friends. Everybody and everything else, I have to release right now. Maybe for good.

So, like I said, I wrote the e-mail this morning and blind-carbon-copied everyone who had planned to join Rex and me on the banks of the Yellowstone in March:

> *Dear friends:*
> *There's no other way to say it except just to say it: Rex*

and I will not be marrying. I will not sugarcoat this. It was his decision, he does not want to be with me, and thus, I do not want to be with him. It's over. There is literally nothing else to say about it. So I won't.

If you feel as though you must respond, feel free to do so. Please do not hold it against me if I don't reply. I'm sure you will understand. Soon enough, I hope, there will be happier times. I look forward to seeing you then.

Love,

Jo-Jo

I shut down the browser and put the computer to sleep, and then, as I walked past an accepted wedding invitation I'd received five days ago, enclosed in a belated Christmas card—thank you, Ed and Kathy Zucker, and sorry I won't be seeing you—and the invoice for the wedding cake (your basic three-tiered beauty, only with light pink buttercream instead of the fluffy white stuff in a basket-weave design, and strawberry filling inside), at long last I was fully broken open.

I ran to the bedroom with brimming eyes, flung myself atop the bed and ugly-cried myself to sleep, while my sweet Cholly stood by and nuzzled my hands.

I cried over a man.

Over a wedding.

Over a stupid social tradition.

I should have seen this coming so long ago and gotten myself out of it before now.

I AWOKE HOURS LATER TO THE INSISTENT HUM OF MY PHONE, buzzing on the end table. I felt like warmed-over poo. Hair knotted, eyes puffy and glazed, that sandman tingle that comes from not knowing whether it's night or day. I pulled the phone close. *L to the M*, it said. Larry

Morelli. Not the caller I expected, but then again, I didn't really have any expectations.

"Larry," I answered.

"God, you sound awful."

"Happy New Year to you, too, buddy."

He laughed, the Larry Morelli answer to all uncomfortable moments. "Sorry, Jo. I got your e-mail."

"Yeah?"

"I'm sorry. I really am."

"Thanks."

He cleared his throat, the Larry Morelli answer to all discussions he'd rather not have.

"We need to talk," he said.

"OK, go."

"Face to face."

"When?"

"What are you doing now?"

I sat up, my senses attenuated at last. "Now?"

"Yeah, I'll meet you over at City Brew. Twenty minutes?"

"This better be good," I said.

He cleared his throat again. "OK. Twenty minutes."

"Make it thirty," I said. He agreed, and we hung up. For maybe a minute, I sat on the edge of the bed, my head hanging, and let my thoughts find some kind of order before I hit the shower, hiding my hair under a plastic cap. Nothing to be done about my baggy eyes on such short notice. Not that there was anyone to impress. I slid my hair back into a ponytail and hid it yet again under a Mighty Jo's Gym ball cap. A pullover covered my sleep-crumpled T-shirt. Yoga pants, sneakers, and I was good to go.

Well, twenty-eighteen, I can't say you're impressing me much so far.

Can't say I'm expecting much, either.

Mr. Blue Sky

Let's get a few things straight ...

As THE KIDS SAY, yo, wassup? You know, that's why being a kid is such a relatively short portion of an average-length human life. They say and do a lot of lovable, dumb stuff. Yet with a little maturity and good luck and a reasonable dental plan, they can emerge from their youth relatively unscathed and get on with the business of being fully realized adults. That can sometimes be a lot tougher than being young, especially when you factor in such inscrutable things as careers and overactive bladders. But adulthood is also where you realize your greatest potential, generally speaking. Show me someone who topped out in childhood, and I'll show you someone who gets laughed at by everybody else at the high school reunion.

So, then, let's talk about these things in the context of Miss Middlebury and Mister Travers, who seem to be following entirely different trajectories after their New Year's Eve tongue-wrestling session.

I'm not one for too much exposition, but as someone who's been watching these two a lot longer than you have, I can offer a bit of context.

About Jo-Jo Middlebury, I'll say this: She's come by her wariness honestly, if not entirely innocently. What I mean is that she entered this world with a shitty set of cards—this happens, and I don't want to hear one word about a "master plan," because you do not have time for me to dissect and dispel the many layers of that notion. Anyway, she's come far from her beginnings, even if the journey has been more of a squiggle than a straight line. As the song goes, regrets, she's had a few. But she's a good human, as humans go. When it comes to those she cares about, she's loyal to the core. She's also got a good work ethic. And she makes a mean eggplant parmesan.

And young Mr. Travers there has also come by his worldview in an organic way. Good parents who instilled their morals and values in him, and then encouraged him to question them and redefine his own. Good, if isolated, upbringing (that tends to be the case with only children). He has a mind, and he's used it, and for the most part he's kept it open. He cares deeply about the people in his life, be they transient or permanent. Keeps in touch with former students. Calls his parents. Likes cats. He's maybe more idealistic than most people of his age and experience, and that can be seen in some quarters as weakness. I don't think he's weak. I think he's a man in progress. And Linus, like Jo-Jo, is a good human. Would that they all were.

A long time ago (in your concept of time, but nothing more than a fraction of a second in mine), there was a fellow named Johann Wolfgang von Goethe, a writer of some renown. He committed something to paper that I like to recite, because it gets close to the universal truth:

"Whatever you can do, or dream you can do,
Begin it. Boldness has genius, power, and
magic in it."

I daresay that young Travers is embracing that ethos. It'll be interesting to see what comes of it, because Jo-Jo Middlebury isn't buying boldness or much of anything else. Not yet, anyway. Maybe not ever.

Linus

Dial M for moron

Siri came through.

The Y. Out.

LA Fitness. (In Billings?) Out.

Body Builders. Out.

Curves. Maybe. I think those things are franchises you can buy into.

Mighty Jo's Gym. *Ding ding ding ding ding!* Call off the dogs. The hunt is over.

I didn't even need to plug the address into the GPS. Knew exactly where it was. In no time, I was cruising up Grand Avenue until I pulled into the location next to the paint store and found the parking lot empty.

A parking lot to a gym empty on New Year's Day?

I saw a sign on the door:

Due to lying contractors, our Grand Opening has been delayed. We apologize for the inconvenience. You deserve the best.

Damn. That must have cost her a shit-ton of money.

Of course, my second thought went to wondering whom she used. If I had to venture a guess, I'd say Rockin' Robiskey Builders was at the top of the suspect list. That crew and lying contractors were synonymous. The very definition, you could say.

Precisely why I'd gone into the business. There are only so many times you can say "I could have done a way better job" before people start taking you up on it, you start actually doing it, and then realize you like doing it and can get paid for it.

And then it dawned on me: *She needs a contractor! I'm a contractor!*

Sometimes I'm slow on the uptake.

I went back to Siri and asked for contact information on Mighty Jo's Gym (gosh, that's a cute name).

Can I just say that Steve Jobs's golden-voiced, simulated servant makes life livable? Would that be too much of an overstatement?

I called and a message came up after the first ring: *Thank you for calling Mighty Jo's Gym. Come to our Grand Opening on November nineteen, twenty-seventeen, and enter to win a lifetime membership. For operating hours, Press One. For personal training services, Press Two. For—*

I hung up. She needed to update her message. But yeah, that was her. That sultry voice was burned on my brain.

But wait. I still needed to talk to her.

I dialed again.

Thank you for calling Mighty Jo's Gym. Come to our Grand Opening on November nineteen, twenty-seventeen, and enter to win a lifetime membership. For operating hours, press One. For personal training services, press Two. For weight loss management and nutrition classes, press Three. For Zumba, Step, and other cardio class schedules, press Four. For Yoga or Pilates class schedules, press Five. For all other inquiries, press Zero.

Finally. I tapped the 0.

Another ring. *You've reached Jo-Jo Middlebury, owner and operator of Mighty Jo's Gym. Please leave your name, number, and a brief message—and I mean brief—and I will return your call as soon as possible. Thank you.*

Following the beep, I spoke. "Hello, Jo-Jo. I mean, Miss Middlebury. *Ms.* Middlebury. My name is Linus Travers. Um, I'm an independent contractor and I saw that the opening of your gym has been delayed, and if you're in need of a new contractor, I'd like to offer myself to you. I mean, I'd like to offer my services. A business proposal. You can look me up. I mean Google me. As a contractor, because that's what I am. I've got top reviews on Yelp, Angie's List, the Billings Better Business Bureau. ... OK, I made that last one up. There is no Billings Better Business Bureau. At least I don't think there is. Shit, this isn't brief. Here's my number: Seven-nine-four, one-nine-seven-eight. Thank you."

I closed out the call and flung the phone over my shoulder into the cargo seat, where it hit the passenger window. I'm pretty sure that was the sound of a screen cracking. Then I wiped the sweat from my forehead and banged said forehead on the steering wheel a few times before climbing over the seat to retrieve my phone— screen intact, thank goodness; the cracking was a CD jewel case on the floor of the back seat.

I WAS BARELY IN MY HOUSE WHEN AMANDA CALLED. My ex-wife. My gut took a jab when I saw her name on the screen, but I answered with a cheerful, "Happy New Year!"

"Hey, Linus," she said. "So Bryce and I are going to finish the basement and we found some stuff that belongs to you."

Do you know how many times I asked—no, offered—to finish the basement?

"What kind of stuff?" I asked.

"How should I know? It's all in boxes. Anyway, you need to pick them up."

"You can't drop them off here, on your way to … wherever?" I already knew the answer to that. Amanda avoided the South Side as if it were the portal to hell.

"You pretty much answered your own question, didn't you?"

I did a face/palm and wearily rubbed my eyes. This was what life was always like with Amanda. She never asked for anything. She either demanded or insisted. Two months before we divorced, we replaced the roof and all the windows in our house following a storm that produced golf-ball-sized hail. Roofs are beyond my pay grade, so we called in a buddy of mine for the roof and I threw some work to another buddy for the windows. We'd decided to go ahead and replace all the windows because it was an older house, and we knew energy-efficient windows would lower our monthly bill. All worked out well, except I didn't get to enjoy them. Terms of the divorce: She got the house; I got the roof and window bills in lieu of alimony since we didn't have kids. Why? Because Amanda insisted. Demanded. Big-time pooch screwing, but it got me out of the entanglement faster, and that's what I wanted. You can't move on without, you know, moving on. But sometimes in the haste to move on, you capitulate to things that someone with a cool and collected mind would never accept. Yet another casualty of divorce, albeit temporary if you're lucky.

I tried to stifle an exasperated sigh but failed. "What's a good time for me to get them?"

"Whenever," she said. "Just let Bryce know when you're on your way."

I bristled every time the name was uttered. Like hearing a taboo word. Did I mention that Bryce was our accountant? Whom Amanda is now married to? After she slept with him? While we were still married?

"I'd rather not interact with him," I said.

"Fine," she said with a huff. "I see you haven't grown a spine yet."

I burned with equal parts humiliation and anger. "I didn't realize that exercising one's boundaries was synonymous with spinelessness." I shook my head. "And here I thought you were calling to wish me well." I said it more to me than to her.

Without warning, she switched gears. "You go to Larry and Jennifer's party last night? I miss them, you know."

"They're still your friends," I said. "You could call them. I'm sure they'd be happy to hear from you."

"They're *your* friends, Linus. They were from day one. And Jennifer thinks I'm the Queen Bitch now."

"I've got another call coming in," I lied. "Have a good year. I mean that. I wish you the best."

"See you, Linus."

I stared at my phone. How does the progression from being madly in love (her words at the beginning of our relationship) to not giving you a second thought happen? Is there one specific trigger? Is it a snowball effect? Or, in Amanda's case, had she never been in love with me but rather with the idea of being in love? Jenn has long insisted that I was in love with the idea of being married to Amanda rather than being in love with Amanda. And Amanda was right about Jenn not thinking too highly of her since the divorce. But, hey, I was trying to be nice. Maybe that was my problem. Maybe I really was spineless.

As if it had sprouted to life, the phone started vibrating in my hand to the tune of "What's New Pussycat" while I was still staring at it, causing me to jump and nearly drop it. After fumbling to regain my grip, I tapped the screen.

"Hello?" I said.

"Is this Linus?" asked a female voice.

"It is."

"This is Jo-Jo Middlebury. What can you do for me?"

Jo-Jo

From now on, the choice is mine

I PULLED INTO THE PARKING LOT OF THE CITY BREW ON 27TH STREET, and Larry's truck was already there, which meant I could predict the rest. He'd be inside the coffee shop, perched at a high-top table facing the door, which wouldn't matter a bit because he'd have his head buried in his phone. A bigger waste of time I've never seen. And he'd be wearing straight-legged, dark blue jeans and a shaker sweater over a heather gray T-shirt, and loafers. Hair combed. Clean shaven.

Sure enough. I was dead-on. All of it. You'd think he was posing for a *People* magazine lifestyle shoot rather than recovering from a New Year's Eve bash.

"Boo," I said, sliding onto the chair opposite him.

He jumped like a spooked cat, his iPhone fumbling across the table. I caught it as it cascaded over my edge.

"Shit, Jo-Jo," he said. "I didn't see you."

I passed the phone across the distance. "You wouldn't have seen a linebacker flying at your head."

"Luckily, that's almost never a concern here," he said. I laughed. He laughed. It was the "almost" that made it funny.

"I got you the usual," he said, sliding a tall latte cup toward me. Triple skinny vanilla.

"Thank you."

"Coffee for those who don't want a lot of calories but do want to make four bathroom runs overnight."

"Calories nothing," I said. "I dislike whole milk."

"Of course," he said. "I forgot."

Every once in a while, Larry and I have an exchange and it's ... awkward. We move into the moment and right back out of it, but there's also this awareness that he gets me, and because he gets me I am by definition vulnerable. I don't like being vulnerable. And so when I feel those moments come on, I try to move us onto another track.

"So, Big L, what do you want to talk about? Because I have a long day ahead of me. Got resolutions to break. That sort of thing."

Larry leaned in. Clutched his hands in front of him. Gave me that look. You know the look. The *I'm-going-to-back-in-to-what-I-have-to-say-here-because-I'm-uncomfortable* look.

"How'd you like the party?"

"Great. It was great."

"Yeah?"

"Considering my fiancé just dumped me? Sure, it was a blast," I said.

"You weren't there for long."

"Well, as I just said ..."

"Right," he said. "Sorry."

"Don't be."

I sipped my coffee. He sipped his. He made popping noises with his lips and looked around the coffee shop as if it were newly discovered ground.

"That it?" I asked.

"You kissed somebody at midnight," he said.

Shit, I had forgotten about that.

"Yes," I said. "Yes, I did."

"Interesting choice, considering."

Considering *what*? The whole damn room was full of people kissing people. Conformity isn't exactly my thing, but neither is looking out of place at a social engagement. And I'm pretty sure Larry didn't witness it, because he and Jennifer came out of the kitchen just in time to say goodbye to me, which was approximately five seconds after I put my tongue in that guy's mouth. Which, by the way, was none of Larry's business, and I was pretty sure he knew that.

"Jealousy doesn't become you, Lawrence," I said.

He flicked a straw wrapper at me. "Don't call me that. And it's not jealousy. It's not even concern, at least not for me."

"Oh, really? Then why are we here?"

"It's just that the guy you kissed, well, he tends to get carried away."

"What do you mean?"

"Like, he was grilling Jenn about you," he said.

"What do you mean, grilling?"

"Not in a creepy way, just … interested. But the thing is … how do I say this?" Larry cupped his hands behind his head and laced his fingers, and he leaned back, buying time. "He's a good dude. Nice. A little too nice sometimes. And … naïve, I guess. I don't mean anything derogatory by that. It's just—"

"Larry?"

"Yeah?"

"It didn't mean anything. I kissed him and I left. That's it. The end."

Larry let out a blast of air. What was he so relieved about? "Well, I'll tell him that."

"Please do."

"OK."

He rose from his seat, only to grab his glutes as he cringed. "You OK, Lar?"

"I ran two miles this morning."

I rolled my eyes. "Well, that was predictable."

He scowled. "What? Just because I made the same New Year's resolution everyone makes? Besides, your damn gym isn't open yet."

I didn't have to say anything because he already realized the insensitivity of his remark, albeit a second too late. "Shit, Jo-Jo," he said. "I'm really sorry. I'm an asshole."

He was, too. Sorry, that is. I could tell. And while his comment certainly was asshole-ish, it also wasn't like Larry. Because here's the thing: In the same way he knew where all my scars were, I knew where all his were.

I peered at him. "You sure you're OK?"

"Never better," he said. "Just sore. From running."

I LEFT THE COFFEE SHOP FEELING—I don't know—*buoyed*, if such a feeling was possible given the general disrepair of my life. Once we'd cleared the decks of the kissing thing and his stupid utterance about my gym, the coffee and the time with Larry had a restorative effect. I got some bucking up from a good friend, and I shored up my comfort with what I can and cannot control.

Rex is gone, and good riddance to him.

The wedding is gone, and while I'd convinced myself I badly wanted it, that event is clearly not intended for me.

I have my life, and I have a decision to make about my gym (a sad one—I think it's time to give it up, if for no other reason than it's part of a shitty year I'd just as soon forget). I have all the agency in the world to call the shots on those two things. That's enough for me. It ought to be enough for anyone.

I settled into the car seat and checked the phone I'd left in the cup holder. A message awaited, from a number I didn't recognize. I put it on speakerphone.

"Hello, Jo-Jo. I mean, Miss Middlebury. Ms. *Middlebury. My name is Linus Travers. Um, I'm an independent contractor and I saw that the opening of your gym has been delayed, and if you're in need of a new contractor I'd like to offer myself to you. I mean, I'd like to offer my services. A business proposal. You can look me up. I mean Google me. As a contractor, because that's what I am. I've got top reviews on Yelp, Angie's List, the Billings Better Business Bureau. ... OK, I made that last one up. There is no Billings Better Business Bureau. At least I don't think there is. Shit, this isn't brief. Here's my number: Seven-nine-four, one-nine-seven-eight. Thank you."*

A contractor, huh?

Not just a contractor, but one who called me and rambled. Unsolicited. One who wasn't returning my call a week and a half after I placed it. One I hadn't fired. Not yet, anyway. A corny one, too.

OK, Linus Travers, let's hear it.

I tapped the call back. Three rings, and he picked up and greeted me with "hello."

"Is this Linus?" I asked.

"It is."

"This is Jo-Jo Middlebury. What can you do for me?"

A pause. A long one.

"Hello?" I asked.

"So much," he said at last. "I can do so much for you. Specifically, I can get your gym open."

"How did you know I own a gym? And that it's not finished?"

He didn't answer the questions. "You can investigate my work with a simple Google search. Who'd you go with before? Rockin' Robiskey?"

I was dumbstruck. "How did you know *that*?"

"I know things." The way he said it was disarming. It wasn't cocky, and it wasn't a bullshit line. He said he knew things, and I didn't even have to ask myself whether I believed him. I did.

"I'm listening," I said.

"So let me paint a picture here," he said. "You can't ever get Robiskey's people on the phone. They're late with everything. Their markups on material, not to mention the labor costs, are killing you. You're one of about fifteen projects they have going at once and—"

"Eighteen," I said, remembering their lead guy Dirk Dolan— seriously, that was his name—mansplaining how the contracting business works.

"Eighteen," he repeated. "And most days, you feel like you're the last of their priorities."

"You do know things, Mr. Travers. So I ask again: What can you do for me?"

"I want you to know this," he said. "When I'm working for you, you're my only client. You tell me what you want done and I do it, and I'm marking up materials only ten percent—"

Ten percent? I was incredulous. "Are you Santa Claus?"

"I'm Linus, Miss Middlebury, and Santa Claus has a rather poor work ethic, if you ask me."

Linus Travers was a funny guy. Sort of. Good for him. But if I'm going to do this gym (and wasn't I thinking just a minute ago that I won't?), I need a get-stuff-done contractor. Whether he was funny or not was immaterial. Could this guy back all of this up? That was the pertinent question. Dirk Dolan talked a good game, too. Made me laugh. Broke my heart. And I fired his ass.

"As I was saying," he continued, "I think I can have you open by the beginning of February, depending on what needs to be done. If that's what you want."

I started the car, checked the mirrors, and put it into reverse, cutting a crisp line into the parking lot and heading for the street. "Well, Linus, here's the deal. I'm going to check out your work. If I like what I see, I'll be in touch again soon. And you better be right about what you're telling me. Because I'll hold you to it."

"I'd expect no less."

"Bye."

I hung up. I aimed the car down the hill on 27th Street, Billings below me, in tones of brown and gray from bare trees and cloudy sky and dirty snow pushed to the sides of the street.

Happy New Year?

I hadn't thought so twenty-four hours ago. But if my gym can be open and ready to go by the beginning of February, I might be willing to reconsider.

Mr. Blue Sky

It isn't up to me

He's a surprising young man, this Linus Travers, isn't he?

By that, I mean this: Who you are and what you grow into are not static factors that you receive on the cosmic assembly line, such as it is. When you come into the world, you are both a blank canvas and a being with a history. You inherit a story on the first day of your Earth-born life, and from the first moment, you begin to process the coding of that inherited story. You absorb it. You add to it. You pass it on.

For example, maybe your mother came from a family with thirteen other children, and you figure out that no matter how much food is on the table, she eats with an arm around her plate, protecting it. Maybe your grandfather on your father's side returned home from World War II and would inexplicably disappear for entire weekends, either down in the basement with the lights off or on random road trips where he was unreachable. The point is that these things—these occurrences that pre-date you—become part of who you are. This happens because you notice the details, because they're told to you in stories, and because those stories get folded into your consciousness. And they affect you, sometimes in overt ways and sometimes in subtle ways that you don't even realize. As you make your own way through the world, your own experiences and impressions enter the mix, and you become who you are, and you keep becoming as you add new experiences and information. Everything matters, but childhood matters most of all, because that's where the big imprints get made. Simple fact.

So, anyway, back to Linus ...

Linus wasn't what I would call a confident child. Let's just say he had an overdeveloped interior life. (Cue the chorus: *"He had an overdeveloped interior life."* Man, I loved *Police Squad*. Look it up.) He didn't have other siblings, and his father, an Air Force pilot, moved the family a lot, so the burden was pretty much on Linus to figure out how to assimilate into new places and among new faces. And when he wasn't doing that, he was by himself much of the time. Between you and me, they didn't do him any favors with that first name. That's a lot of teasing, and a little bit of that nonsense goes a long way.

But Linus had an ace in the hole. Wherever his family roamed, Linus had a library card and an easy way with himself. He enjoyed his own company, and as long as he had something new to learn, he was content, if not happy.

As far as happiness goes; maybe later, when I'm not in the middle of a *Twilight Zone* marathon, we can explore the limitations of what humans consider happiness to be. Believe me, you're missing a lot.

Anyway, what Linus learned, over time, is that while human interactions sometimes baffled him, he could always rely on his brain. So all that confident talk to Jo-Jo, that was Linus's way with his work coming to the fore. He knows what he can do. And what he can do, as it turns out, is right in line with what Jo-Jo Middlebury needs at this juncture, and not just in terms of contracting services. (No, I don't mean *that*—sheesh!)

I reiterate that I played no role in any of this. And neither did who or what you think—The Guy Upstairs. Her Holiness. The Supreme Being. The Source. The I Am. The Almighty. Big Gorilla. It's nothing like that, by the way. It might even baffle you to know that it's not even all that lofty. More like ... *simple*. Technically, it's not even an *it*. Or a he or a she. I get your need to personify and assign a gender role. Hence my moniker. The point is that this ain't Fonzie turning the jukebox on and off with his fist. You're in a universe that sustains you, you have the collective knowledge of all who've come before, and you have your own boundless curiosity and possibilities. You have everything you need.

I can tell you this, though. Linus may get a chance to see Jo-Jo again because of what he said to her. Good for him. And although he can hang a mean drywall, I don't know if he's ready for the rest of what he's imagining. Because with that interior life came a fertile imagination. And sometimes that admirable quality betrays him. Jo-Jo is nobody's project. She is her own sovereign being, with her own ideas about who she is and where she's headed.

Pass the popcorn.

Linus

It's not what you think

I KILLED IT—*killed it*—in my phone call.

I mean that as a good thing. Unlike Bumbling Moron Linus who'd left the voicemail, Actual Linus was calm and cool when Jo-Jo called back. I made my pitch. I told it like it was. I won a meeting with her, because she called me again that night and said, "OK, let's sit down and talk about this."

And I was so primed. Since our last chat, I'd imagined us sitting here at the City Brew on 27th Street, at this very table, face to face. She'd give me her numbers. I'd give her my numbers. She'd tell me her problems. I'd tell her the solutions. And by the time we emptied our cups, we'd be shaking hands on the deal.

I had arrived ten minutes early with my iPad in tow, armed with before-and-after photos of previous jobs and comparison rate sheets and calendar projections, plus a tad extra Aqua Velva behind the ears. I even ironed my dress shirt and didn't burn it. Yet another one that brought out my eyes. (Or so Jennifer said when I bought it with her.) So it was minus-two degrees outside and I should have been wearing a thermal shirt underneath it, or should have ditched it in favor of flannel. But I didn't want to look stocky. Besides, the super-something-latte I'd just ordered would warm me up. As would Jo-Jo's gratitude at what I was going to be able to do for her.

She strode in, five minutes late, dressed in a silver puffy coat and matching wool hat, scarf, and gloves, all that looked knitted by hand and all a deep wine hue. Her hair was long and black and straight, and I instantly yearned to feel it on my chest, swishing against my skin.

She approached my table first; I was the only person sitting alone. I stood up, positioning myself so the tabletop hid my … er, zipper fly.

"Linus?" she asked. That voice. In the spirit of the season, it was like hot caramel poured over vanilla ice cream.

I smiled and extended my hand. "Hi, Jo-Jo. Nice to meet you again."

Her brow crinkled. And then my heart plummeted, because I knew I'd blown it with just one word.

"Again?" she asked.

And then Bumbling Moron Linus pummeled Actual Linus, who was apparently too beautiful to live. "Oh. Uh … Well, you know, we—um …"

She peered closer, closing the space between us. Did a retinal scan of my face poised for a mugshot, consulted her mental databank, and then it all fully registered: *New Year's Eve. The kiss.* And her soft, rounded cheekbones became stark and straight as she frowned and nearly hissed.

"Oh my God. You little cockbag."

I recoiled as if she'd slapped my face. "Whoa, now."

"You're … *the guy*. From the party."

"Hang on, Jo-Jo. Let me explain."

"Don't call me Jo-Jo like we know each other. This is really creepy, dude."

"I wasn't trying to be creepy, I was trying to—"

"I told you I was done. Sure, I was a little drunk. But I said it plain and simple, and I meant it. No means no. And now you're *stalking* me?"

"I am not *stalking* you," I said, a little too loudly. A barista glared at us.

"God, this was probably what Larry was trying to warn me about," she said. "I bet you're not even a contractor."

Larry was warning her about me? Why would he do such a thing? What had he said?

"I really am. Look, it's not what you think."

Jo-Jo laughed. Out loud. In that condescending way, the kind that makes you shrink to the floor and want to scurry away like a cockroach.

"It's not what you think!" she mimicked and laughed again, shaking her head.

Now I was pissed. What was it that Jenn had said? *She's hard to know.*

"OK, fine," I said. "I may have inquired about you. And maybe it was inappropriate to approach you in the way I did, but—"

She turned on her heel and headed for the door. I chased her, rambling on. Because that isn't creepy or stalker-ish at all. "Please listen to me—that doesn't mean I can't help you. I'm totally on the level. I know you're behind schedule. I know you're dealing with a contractor who doesn't give one shit about you or your business. I know I can help you."

We were in the parking lot now, our breath shooting out in rows of steam. A gust of wind bore through every buttonhole of my dress shirt and pricked me like a thousand needles. I could have screamed.

She stopped and faced me, and rolled her eyes around, as if she were calling bullshit.

"Linus," she started.

I leaned forward, hopeful for a change in direction. "Yes?"

"Go fuck yourself," she said, and then she aimed her key at her maroon Subaru, remotely disarming the alarm and unlocking the doors.

"Now that was totally uncalled for," I said. Then I pointed to my pickup truck. "There's mine." She glanced at it and returned to her own. I shouted behind her, "Record the license plates. Look me up. Grill Larry and Jennifer. Google me. Read the reviews on Angie's List. Call the Billings Education Association and check out my record as a schoolteacher. Find out everything you need to know about me."

As she opened the door and slipped into the leather seat, one nanosecond before she slammed the door, I shouted my final words: *"I'm sorry!"*

She started the car and revved the engine.

Another gust of wind practically ripped my shirt off as I folded my arms in straitjacket formation, turned, and headed back inside City Brew, relieved to see that no one had run off with my iPad. The baristas pretended I wasn't there despite their shadowy peripheral glances. *Well, great. I can't ever come back here.* I looked out the window one last time and, to my surprise, Jo-Jo hadn't yet peeled out of the parking lot. She was aiming her phone at my truck, snapping photos.

And with that, I shook off the cold, returned to my table, and packed my things.

Jo-Jo

When will a man be a man?

Right. So I still have this problem: my gym is screwed, and only a contractor can unscrew it if I decide I want it. And I do. I *want* it.

And that little weasel Linus, I don't know what he knows or found out about me in his stalking. But he probably doesn't know that one of my best friends is a cop. Anyway, he insisted that I check him out, and so I put Caroline the cop on it, and she called me a few hours later and said, "Linus Travers. Not a damn thing. Not even a parking ticket, which is just about impossible in this town."

"Thanks, C," I said.

"This guy giving you any trouble?"

"No."

Yes. Maybe. Shit, I don't know.

"I'm sorry about Rex," she said.

"No, you're not."

"No, I'm not," she said. "Let's have lunch soon, OK?"

"Deal."

Caroline had never warmed up to Rex, which underscores her good instincts and my poor ones. I think she tried to be happy for me, the way a friend would, and she knew me well enough to understand that I'd made up my mind. But I could tell. Right after Rex and I got engaged, she and I had a long night of cocktails on the balcony at the 406—the kind of night when I didn't care about that—and she said, in a candid moment, that "he just has this vibe, like he's not in it as far as you are."

"He is," I'd insisted.

"OK," she'd said. "Maybe he just doesn't transmit on my frequency."

Who the hell says something like that? Someone who's being diplomatic about someone she doesn't like, that's who. It's funny how that conversation came charging back into my head not an hour after Rex left. Caroline could sense his lack of commitment. I couldn't. And that sucks.

The thing is, I'm all about the retrospect now. Like, how did it not set off my alarm bells when I couldn't ever find a friend who wanted to double-date with Rex and me? And how is it that every instance of Rex being rude or dismissive to restaurant servers and toll booth attendants and anybody else who has a job of serving the public—how is it that all of those things never registered with me in the moment but now torpedo my head, unwelcome and yet crystal-clear? He called every last one a shit job, for chrissakes.

I'm a fool.

I'm just not as big a fool as Linus Travers seems to think I am.

AT THREE A.M. IT BECAME OBVIOUS SLEEP WASN'T GOING TO STICK. I flopped around in bed, my brain zooming at a hundred million miles an hour, where no thought could be held for more than five seconds, and no prospect of sleep was present unless I got up and forced myself to concentrate on a task.

Fine.

I slid out of bed. Cholly kept sleeping, the inconsiderate shit.

I fired up the coffee pot and roused my laptop from its sleep.

"OK, Linus Travers," I said, "let's see what you've got."

Linus Travers Contracting Co. had a 5.0 rating on Yelp, which is astounding, because the average Yelp user exists solely to eviscerate others. Or so it seems.

> *Perfect. Absolutely perfect. Started the job when he said he would and finished three days early. My new bathroom is pristine and beautiful and exactly what I wanted.*

And this:

> *Linus Travers explained the scope of the job in detail, breaking it down by stage and by cost. And at the end, he returned $2,000 to me and said he'd come in under budget. I've never heard of such a thing.*

And this:

> *The most honest, straightforward contractor I've ever worked with. And a guy you'd want your daughter to meet.*

I doubted that. The guy might be God's gift to backsplashes, but he still came up deficient in my book.

Which made me think: the guy said he was a teacher, right? If he was a bona fide creep, maybe that's why he wasn't a teacher anymore. I realized I'd have to wait to call the Billings Education

Association if I had reason to, but in the meantime I figured there had to be some kind of virtual trail.

I logged on to my Facebook account, with my seven friends and no profile picture. The only reason I established an account was to satisfy Rex, who said we could share our wedding and honeymoon photos with his 723 friends.

I looked up Linus Travers. His page was buttoned up tight. I could see only his profile picture, one where only his eyes were visible, rising up behind the head of a tuxedo cat with a cute little white spot on its nose.

I don't know if this is a sexist thing, but I don't think I've ever known a male cat owner who wasn't weird. OK, it's definitely a sexist thing, but that's my experience. Or maybe all cat owners are weird.

Anyway, a couple of posts down on the search results was one from a girl named Delia Mayes, and there, in the picture, was Linus Travers, staring at a cake, a bunch of high school kids ringed around him, and he had his hands clasped together in front of his mouth, and he was bowing slightly. She wrote:

> *Said goodbye to my most favorite teacher ever. Mr. Travers is the best. I hate math, but he made it fun. And awwwww, he even cried. BEST OF LUCK, MR. TRAVERS!!!*

I don't suppose creepy-ass teachers get going-away parties. I clicked on the photo, bringing it up and enlarging it on my screen. The dude's cheeks were red. And, sure enough, that was either a glare or tears in his eyes.

I hoped it was a glare.

I do not want to think well of this guy.

Linus

Can we get back to me?

I ENTERED LARRY AND JENNIFER'S HOUSE A FEW DAYS LATER, still ashamed but ready to see my friends again. I sat at the kitchen table and buried my head in my hands after banging it on the tabletop a couple of times. Jennifer had already set a place for me and loaded a plate with bacon and scrambled eggs. Larry was reading and responding to e-mails on his tablet, trying to keep his necktie from dipping into the Cholula he'd dumped on his eggs. He'd already mistaken the mug-sized pitcher of maple syrup for his coffee cup and took a sip from it, squinching his face in recoil. Charlie was busy cutting his Eggo waffles into different geometric shapes, announcing them as he did so before forking each one into his mouth. "Square! Rectangle! Parallelogram!"

Jenn chortled. "Most kids try to shape their waffles into Mickey Mouse heads. My kid does advanced geometry."

"Maybe he'll be a math teacher when he grows up," I said, slightly lifting my head and peeking at Charlie, whose smile revealed a mouthful of waffle. I buried my head again.

"I don't want to be a teacher," Charlie said.

"No?" asked Jenn. "What do you want to be?"

"A villain."

Even Larry looked up and eyed him quizzically with the rest of us. "A what?" he asked.

Before Charlie could repeat his dastardly plan, Jenn prodded him to get on with his routine before the bus came—brush and floss, tie shoes, finish filling his backpack, disperse kisses, and out the door. As he scooted out of the kitchen, Jenn clarified: "We watched *Despicable Me 3* again the other day. He wants the gadgets."

Larry shook his head. "Kid's going to be a computer hacker by age ten. I just know it."

"They're in demand these days," I offered. "He could make some good coin."

"So how badly did you mess up?" Jenn asked without warning of a subject change. Larry went back to his tablet. I'd mentioned my run-in with Jo-Jo when I texted Jenn the previous night, which prompted the breakfast invitation.

"On a scale of one to ten? Thirty-five," I said.

She winced and tossed me some sugar packets for my coffee. "I'll bet it wasn't that bad."

I ripped and unloaded all three packets into my mug at once. "She accused me of stalking her. Called me creepy. And a cockbag."

Larry laughed. Jennifer shot him a glare, one I'd seen before in recent months. Like she couldn't believe she married *him*. "Oh, come on. That's funny," he protested.

"It's very Jo-Jo," Jenn said. "Over-reactive. Dramatic. Angry at the world."

"She is not angry at the world," Larry said. "For God's sake, Rex dumped her four days ago. Just two months before their wedding. How would you feel?"

Rex? The guy's name was Rex? And he dumped her? Well, that explained the kiss.

"I had a cat named Rex when I was a kid," I blurted. "T-Rex, actually. He caught dragonflies in midair with his teeth, the little feline freak."

No one seemed to have heard me, which was probably a good thing.

Regardless of the guy's name, I hated him for hurting Jo-Jo.

Jenn began to clear the table in a huff, cups and plates clinking with slightly extra force. "Look, I'm not saying she deserved it, but really, what chance at happiness did they have when she's so reluctant to trust?"

"You don't understand," Larry said. I, on the other hand, was starting to. Maybe she wasn't mad at me but at the world. Then again, maybe at me, too.

"Can we get back to me for a sec?" I asked. Not out of selfishness, but as a way to defuse the smoggy tension.

"Just once I'd like you to defend me with the same conviction you do her," said Jenn, ignoring my request—and me—altogether.

"You don't need defending," said Larry.

"Right," she said. "Because you're a clueless moron." And with that she stomped out of the kitchen.

Larry and I exchanged red-faced glances. He shrugged and shook his head in exasperation. "Sorry about that, man."

I paused for a second to let the dust settle. "Do you think she was overreacting?"

"Look, it's just that you kind of undermined me," Larry said. "I told her you're cool, and then you track her down and offer yourself up for her? It may not be stalking, but it was a little too … contrived."

"I meant Jenn."

Larry glowered in a way I'd never seen before. Like a snarling animal. I had never talked about their marriage with him. It wasn't my business. And Larry was confirming that.

Maybe Jo-Jo wasn't my business, either, but I couldn't help myself. I wanted her to be. Despite it all. Maybe *because* of it all. How messed up is that?

"Just back off, man," Larry said. "Let her go. She doesn't need to be rescued."

I wasn't sure whether he was talking about Jenn or Jo-Jo. But I took a gamble this time.

"She does from that shitty contractor," I said.

"Maybe so, but it's not up to you. Let her make her own mistakes and choices. She's smart. She'll figure it out."

"I told her to Google me so she'd find out that I'm not dangerous."

"Oh, she'll do it," Larry said. "She'll probably have you tailed. Her best friend is a cop. Have you looked under your truck for a tracking device?"

Something about this amused me. I liked the idea of Jo-Jo on the prowl. A cat-and-mouse scenario went through my head. Even turned me on a little. I wondered what she'd found so far.

Larry, however, read my thoughts. "Let it go, man. Seriously. It didn't mean anything."

I knew he was talking about the New Year's Eve kiss. My heart sank.

"Maybe not to her," I said.

"Make it not mean anything to you, either. Just get on with life. Join a dating site or something. Take more cooking classes."

I wondered if that last comment was a dig at my coming over for meals so often.

He looked at his watch and rose from the table. "I've got to go."

He grabbed his wallet, keys, and messenger bag and left.

Approximately one minute later, the door closed—not quite a slam, but not calmly, either. They'd left me alone before, but this time it felt weird. Like I'd intruded. I brought my dishes to the sink, washed and dried them, wiped down the counters and table, put things away, and walked to the stairwell as I put on my coat.

"I'm leaving," I called up.

No answer.

I let myself out.

JENN CALLED ME ABOUT A HALF-HOUR LATER WHILE I WAS HOME, removing the kitchen cabinet doors. Winters were slow as far as jobs went, so it was a good time to finally renovate my own kitchen. Maybe Larry was right. Despite the classes, I hadn't liked cooking much since I'd moved into this house. It wasn't a space that was conducive to cooking. Or eating. Or gathering. The layout was all wrong. Countertops scarce. Cabinets scratched. Linoleum faded and cracking. Lighting and wall color dull. Appliances on the other side of their warranties. No dishwasher.

"Sorry about that," she said.

"About what?" She knew I knew. I decided not to press her unless she volunteered more. She didn't.

"And thank you for cleaning up. That was sweet of you. You wouldn't want to fold laundry, too, would you?"

"I've got nothing else to do."

She sighed. "You're a good husband, Linus." Her tone was wistful. Maybe even envious.

"Not really," I said. "And not a husband anymore, remember?"

"Ask me how many times Larry cleans the kitchen before he leaves for work. Or after he gets home. Or any other time."

"I don't think I will."

"And it's *his* kitchen, too, you know what I'm saying? He uses it almost as much as I do"

I felt the need to point out how much time Larry spends with Charlie, helping him with projects and homework and playing games with him, but I skipped it. Jennifer needed validation and support, not one more man in her life ganging up on her.

I said nothing.

Jenn switched gears again. "Listen, I know it sounds like I'm being catty and mean, but you really do need to stay away from Jo-Jo. She's kind of a train wreck."

"I understand."

"I feel sorry about what happened to her, but it's all the more reason for you to steer clear."

"You're right."

"You deserve better."

"I know." I let a pause linger. "You OK?"

Without hesitation, she replied, "I'm fine."

"Thanks for breakfast," I said. We said our goodbyes and I put the phone down, staring blankly at it.

It didn't mean anything. That seemed to be the conventional wisdom. Larry was spouting it and urging me to move on, though given the ugly scene with Jenn, I couldn't be sure if he was saying it out of conviction or just to clear a problem from his load at home. Jenn said it, and her motivation was as suspect as Larry's. Jo-Jo said it, and she's entitled to feel that way, although more and more I was wondering where her right to kiss me ended and my right to do something about it began. Was I horrible for saying that? Was I selfish? I didn't know.

I guessed I was going to have to keep repeating it to myself—"It didn't mean anything"—until it stuck. Like hitting my hand with a hammer until I didn't feel the pain of it anymore.

Jo-Jo

Past, meet present

I DON'T BELIEVE IN SIGNS, or harbingers, or fate. I believe in what's what—that is, what I can see with my own two eyes, in front of my face, using the fully capable brain I was given.

Even so, I had to shake my head when I found out this guy lives across the street and two houses up from where I grew up. Jo-Jo Middlebury: 211 South 37th Street. Linus Travers: 204 South 38th Street. That's ... well, that's weird, isn't it?

I didn't figure him for a South Sider. He may work with his hands, but he's no blue-collar boy, not with those designer glasses and preppy button-down shirts and that courteous way about him (courteous when he's not being a jerk, that is). I figured him for a big house on the West End, not this little turn-of-the-twentieth-century masonry house. I mean, geez, I *know* this house. Kimberley Crater lived there. Her brother Jerry, too. Jerry Crater. First guy I ever kissed, and what I wouldn't give to have that one back so I could make a different choice.

I stood there on the northeast corner of Highland Park, an easy view to my old house and to his, and I tried to separate the memories that moved in on me from the moxie I was going to need to do the thing I'd come here to do. I felt my nerve crumbling, so I started walking. Straight for Linus Travers's front door.

I saw him through the front window, on his knees, his eyes framed by goggles, as he sanded down the edge of a kitchen cabinet door. I shouldn't have, but I lingered by the window and I gawked, and damn, he had the old Crater house in a state of advanced disrepair. Carpet pulled up, rotted hardwood exposed, old lady Crater's floral wallpaper ripped off, light fixtures hanging askew.

This was a reliable contractor?

I slipped to the side of the window and I gave the door two crisp raps, and then I peeked into the corner of the window and I watched.

Jumpy guy. He scrambled to his feet and took the goggles off, and he brushed the back of his hand against his forehead before ambling across the living room.

I moved to align myself with the doorframe, and I spread my stance like a fighter. Because maybe I'd have to be one. Again.

You know how sometimes there's that little pause—just a tiny, fractional second—between when you flip the switch and when the light comes on? That's what it was like. The door opened, Linus Travers stood there looking plaintively at me for that micro-second, and then he broke into a wide smile that, in another blip, morphed into confusion.

"Jo-Jo," he said.

"Miss Middlebury." I said it firmly, as if I expected formality from other people, but I'm really not that way at all. Strange.

"Miss Middlebury," he repeated. "What are—"

I shifted my weight, front foot to back foot, and back again to the front, and I squared up. "Exactly. What am I doing here? You have a lot of questions, don't you?"

"I don't—"

"Don't answer, dude, just listen. You have to be wondering what I've been doing, what business of yours I've been snooping into, what I must know about you, and why I'm here, at your house. It's not very comfortable, is it?"

Now he was just smiling at me. I didn't expect that. And I damn sure didn't like it.

"Would you like to come in?" he asked.

Disarming. And declined. I set my feet again and looked past his shoulder. A cat, the one I'd seen in his Facebook photo, sauntered past us.

"What's your cat's name?"

"Toby. He's a boy."

"You don't like dogs?" I asked.

"I like dogs just fine."

"But you have a cat."

He looked at me quizzically, as if trying to decode my words. "I like cats more," he said.

I switched gears on him. "I sure hope your other jobs don't look like that," I said, eyeing the mess in the house.

He looked behind him. "It's a work in progress. Want to see the finished parts?"

I went a little slack, which disappointed me. I supposed it wouldn't hurt to check out his handiwork in person. Besides, I have a decent left hook. I stepped inside. And, wow, did it look different from the last time I'd set foot in that place. It looked bigger. Linus took me past the kitchen and living room, which was now completely opened up, down the hall to the bedrooms and bathroom. First, the bathroom. One peek inside and I felt as if I just stepped into a showroom. The tub replaced with a custom walk-in shower, complete with adjustable shower head, a shelf that extended the entire length, and a built-in bench—a *bench!* In a house on the South Side. Amazing. It had sleek subway and accent tiles, vanity with granite countertop and double sinks (how he fit those in was beyond me), soft lighting, and flooring that looked like hardwood but I was pretty sure was laminate. The entire motif was contemporary, with stylish tones of gray and black and slate blue. It looked like a guy's bathroom, yet it also managed to capture feminine appeal with fluffy white towels and artwork of flower bouquets.

I had to concede it. "Well. This is impressive."

"Thanks," he said. "I wanted a fixer-upper. Man, I got one."

I followed him deeper into the house. The hardwood floors snaking through this part of the house had been sanded and refinished, the walls freshly painted in a pleasing light-gray hue, and he added built-ins to the master bedroom.

I didn't want to stay in that bedroom any longer than necessary. I flashed on a memory of Mr. and Mrs. Crater going at it in here, with Kimberley and me busting in on them one summer day when we had to be seven, eight years old. I didn't know what I didn't know back then, but the way Mr. Crater came at us, naked below his T-shirt, red face and neck veins bulging ... I shuddered. I turned and strode down the hallway, back toward the front door, and Linus Travers rambled after me.

"Well, I'll tell you what I know about you," I tossed back over my shoulder at him. "I'm pretty sure you're not a dirtbag criminal—"

"Criminal? Geezus—"

At the door, I turned and faced him again. "Don't get indignant. You don't have that right after the other day."

He hung his head.

"Anyway," I continued, and now he looked up. "I'm pretty sure you can do the work I need done. So here's the deal, Mr. Travers. I will see you tomorrow morning at eight at my gym, and I'll show you the place and the mess those Robiskey jerks have left me with, and you'll tell me what you can do, how quickly you can do it, and what it will cost me. That will be all there is, and once you're done with the job, that will be the end of our business. A simple transaction. Your expertise for my money. Got it?"

"Got it." And he smiled again. *What's his deal?*

"Good," I said.

I turned and I left him there, and I walked back across the park to my car, and I got in and left and didn't look back—at Linus Travers, or anything else I once knew.

THE WHOLE WAY HOME, despite my best effort to fight it off, I couldn't get my head out of those two South Side city blocks I knew so well and yet hadn't been to in years, not until Linus Fricking Travers insinuated himself into things. It seemed to me that memory is random and unreliable, because the things I didn't want to think about came to me insistently in a mishmash of times and attitudes.

I'd been out of there for good since my mom died, and believe me, I was never going back. Hell, I almost didn't go back once I saw the guy's address, but I sucked it up because nobody's going to put me on an awkward footing without it coming right back at him.

The thing is, I spent a whole semester twenty years ago balancing college classes with daily visits from my dorm room to that unhappy home because I thought Mom at least deserved a loving goodbye. I bore it. For her. But I'm done now, and have been for a long time.

Three bedrooms, one bathroom, and three girls—four, including Mom—hashing it out for space. My sister Carla and I would double up when Mom would take in a boarder, which was pretty much most of the time, and those guys—they were *always* guys—were varying degrees of trouble, but the trouble part was the constant. Should I start with the scraggly old man who'd run his hands across my eleven-year-old ass, the one I learned not to turn my back on? Or the smooth-talking young construction worker who lured my other sister Debby off to California, land of milk and honey and fortune, until she called a week later, alone and scared in Modesto, and Mom ponied up bus fare home? Or maybe the last one, the one who married Mom in her final days and took everything—the house and the car and the savings account, scant as it was—when she passed on. That hurt, because Mom had truly loved him and had truly hoped we would, too. We didn't, of course. We had seen him for what he was. What can I say about Mom except that she was a good woman with bad judgment. At least she was there. It's more than I can say for our old man, wherever he ended up.

When Mom passed, I had no legal standing, and by then Debby was in Alaska and Carla was in the cemetery after her overdose. I told Mom's husband that I'd slit his throat given the chance.

He believed me. And he should have, because I might well have done it.

One thing I've learned, though, is that justice isn't necessarily mine to dispense. I hope that guy gets what he has coming, one way or another, but I have my own life and my own problems.

Let God sort it out, I'd say, if I believed in a god.

But I don't. I can't. I only know what I know.

I know I found my way out of there.

I know I'm stronger than Mom ever was.

I know if you come at me, you better bring everything you've got, because I won't lie down.

I know Linus Travers better be what he says he is.

I'm all out of trust.

Mr. Blue Sky

Between stimulus and response ...

GOOD FOR JO-JO, stepping out of her comfort zone (and into Linus's), and good for Linus, exercising proper boundaries, especially given that he was showing off his bedroom. But he has a right to be proud of his work. And Jo-Jo needed to see the love and care Linus puts into a project. He transforms spaces into sanctuaries. Or maybe I'm being a tad too poetic.

You may want to make something of the coincidence of his living in her old neighborhood. As if Linus, address and all, was put into her path in order for Jo-Jo to confront those past hurts. I don't see it that way. In her current state of mind, Jo-Jo could have just as easily been triggered by a song on the radio or a scent in a department store. But here's the thing: *Between stimulus and response, man is free to choose.* That's a direct quote from Viktor Frankl, father of existentialism and Holocaust survivor. I bow down to him. Would have loved to work with that guy. What he meant was this: whatever comes at you—loss, illness, abuse, financial hardship, heartbreak, even torture—every one of you has the freedom to choose how you will respond to it. Your choice may not be an entirely conscious one, but nevertheless, there it is. Take the TV show *All in the Family*, for instance. Unlike Archie, Edith Bunker's response to everyone she met, regardless of their religion, color, heritage, age, or social standing, was unconditional love. She *chose* it. Didn't matter where she came from or whom she married.

Now, let's look at Jo-Jo. As the result of her childhood, Jo-Jo has responded to just about every stimulus (i.e., relationship, job, her new gym) by refusing to trust that its outcome will be anything approaching benevolent. Even though she strives for happiness and fulfillment, there's always a part of her heart that she refuses to give because she sees nothing but losses coming from doing so.

Linus, on the other hand, is perhaps too trusting. It's led him to quite a bit of disappointment, but it's also led him to a kind of determined optimism. No matter how many times he gets knocked to the ground, he opts to get back up with his heart fully exposed. This isn't a bad thing, but what he's needed to learn, especially in the wake of his divorce, is boundaries. There's a difference between allowing yourself to be vulnerable and allowing others to walk all over you. Likewise, there's a difference between having healthy boundaries so that others can't take advantage of or hurt you, and having yourself vaulted up like Fort Knox.

These things are all learned, by the way. But that's the beauty of the way your world works. They can be unlearned. And if you pay attention to your thoughts, if you finally admit that the way you've been doing things no longer works for you and never did, then you have the freedom to change it. And if you ask for help, I'll help you. But you need to ask. So few do, because they don't know they can. And it's not my job to make you know. It's my job to love you and be with you even in the moments where you are completely clueless about everything.

Nevertheless, Jo-Jo and Linus both took big steps today, and I'm proud of them.

All in the Family, man. Carroll O'Connor and Jean Stapleton. There's some fine work right there. Cue Louis Armstrong's "What A Wonderful World."

Linus

Promises, shmomises

NOT GONNA LIE. I almost did a happy dance. Not only when I saw her standing in the doorway, but after she left, too. But I've been making a real effort to heed Larry's and Jennifer's admonitions to get Jo-Jo Middlebury out of my head, and a happy dance would have been … well, it would have been too happy. And too hopeful.

She seemed to like the renovations to the house. But she also seemed uncomfortable, and not just from being in Creepy McCreeperson's house. No, she almost had a haunted look about her, as if ghosts lurked in the walls. And maybe they did. This neighborhood has seen its share of hardship. And I've seen my fair share of its insides when I visited the houses of students who needed extra help or whose parents didn't have a car to drive to parent-teacher conferences or to take their kids to school dances or sporting events. I suppose that's one of the reasons I chose a house here rather than central Billings or one of the new turnkeys in the Heights. A house like this one doesn't only have the potential to be reinvented. It has the potential to heal.

I WAS WAITING IN MY TRUCK OUTSIDE THE GYM AT 7:45, the heat on full blast, as I warmed my hands against the Rock Creek coffee cup.

I *love* snow in the morning. I love how silent it is. How gently it falls, unaware that it wreaks havoc with roads and throws out your back when you try to clear a path. How it transforms even a hungry kid's face to happy. As if it has the magical property to make everything right in that child's world the moment she lets a flake fall on her tongue. I love the way it crunches under your boots, how it tingles on your skin, how it lines every limb like fur.

Jo-Jo pulled up at 7:58.

I killed the engine and stepped out of the truck, extending the second cup of coffee I'd brought for her. She shook her head, seemingly oblivious to the snow. "Already had one," she said. I carried it along with my own inside the gym after she unlocked the main doors. We stepped inside and I saw pretty much what my own house looked like—a series of unfinished projects everywhere I looked. Ceilings ripped up. Electrical wires askew. Wall beams exposed. Floors covered in dust and detritus.

Stupid Rockin' Robiskey. Those guys spend thousands on TV advertising, claiming competence, but when it comes down to the hammer meeting the nail, they have no pride and no honor.

"Well," I said as I surveyed the panorama, "this is quite a job they've left you."

"Every time they started something new, they realized something else was done wrong—and they were the ones who did it wrong. Which meant they had to stop what they were doing, undo the last thing to fix it, then patch it back up again. They were supposed to be *finished* by December first. I was supposed to be open on New Year's Day. Do you know how much money I've lost just in the last seven days?" she asked.

"A shit-ton," I said.

"A mega-shit-ton," she corrected.

"I'm sorry."

"It's not your fault."

"I know, but I'm sorry it happened to you. You trusted these guys, and they let you down."

She gave me a pained look, and I remembered what Larry had said about her fiancé dumping her. The rat bastard. What kind of guy does that? How do you sit through months of planning a wedding without having the courage to say it may not be the right thing for you? It occurred to me that she probably lost money there, too—from deposits on catering, photographer, deejay, cake—and thus her gym not opening on time was more than a disappointment. Poor Jo-Jo; her dreams were being trampled left and right.

"Really," I said, "I am so sorry."

Her eyes became glassy, and she looked away, cursing under her breath.

"So what can you do?" she asked in a voice of determination as she avoided eye contact.

I looked around again. "I can fix it. One piece at a time."

"Just you?"

"I have help. They're good, trust me."

I caught my words after they slipped out. *Trust me.* She narrowed her eyes.

"And I can get it done by Presidents' Day, which is the next three-day weekend after MLK Day. A lot of people have that day off. It would be a good day for a grand opening."

"Can you guarantee it?"

"You have my word," I said.

"I've heard that before."

"OK, then what if I tell you this? I don't know what I'm going to find when I poke my head into those ceilings and put those wires together. But I want to do this work for you, Miss Middlebury, because I want your business to open. Will you allow me the chance to do the best I can?"

"For how much?"

I took out my phone, opening the calculator app, and ran some numbers. When I finished, I showed her the total. She raised her eyebrows.

"That's the estimate?" she asked.

"What do you think?"

"How many extra costs do you think will seep in?"

"My hope is that the extras will be under five thousand dollars, if any. But there are usually moves we can make, places where we can blunt the impact. You're leasing the space, right?"

"Yes."

"Well, see, that's good, because any structural problems in the building will be the owner's responsibility. We can do this. I'm sure of it. And I'll work out a payment plan with you, if you want. Also, if I were you, I'd take pictures of all this and post it on every review site you can. You may even want to take Robiskey to small-claims court, because I don't think you should pay them another penny."

She gave me an *Are you for real?* look, and I wondered if I was overselling myself. I knew for a fact my estimate came under what the other crew charged, but a lot of that could be chalked up to their ridiculous markups versus my reasonable ones. Or maybe the offer of the payment plan prompted her skepticism. I just wanted to make life as easy for Jo-Jo as possible because I could tell she needed it.

She hesitated. Then she took in a breath and exhaled forcefully.

"OK, Mr. Travers." She extended her hand. "You're hired. How soon can you start?"

I shook her offered hand, and then I took off my coat. "Now."

Jo-Jo

Hello, New Year

I MAY HAVE UNDERESTIMATED MR. LINUS TRAVERS.

Excuse me if I hedge my bets, though, because it's only one day down, and he's motivated to make me happy on this project, and there's a long way to go. I'm not ready to throw him a parade.

But I may be ready to start hoping I can open this baby on the timetable he outlined.

The first thing he did was show me, from the back of the building to the front door, the order in which he'd get things done. "There's a day coming where we'll step out of these doors," he said, pushing them open with a grand sweep, "and everything behind us will be perfect. *Perfect*."

The second thing he did was get on his phone and make a few calls, and within a half-hour three other guys were tromping around my space, taking measurements, peering into light fixtures—or where the light fixtures will eventually be—and taking inventory of power outlets and the building materials left behind by those worthless cretins at Robiskey. Each one of them—and I'll have to learn their names, I think, but everything moved too fast for me to do so today—greeted me with a handshake and a "pleasure to meet you, Miss Middlebury," and I could certainly get used to that.

As his subcontractors left, Linus saw each to the door and thanked him for his time. He then came back to the middle of the space, set his hands on his hips, fixed a stare on the place, and frowned.

"What?" I asked.

"Do you have a wheelbarrow?"

"No," I said.

"It's OK. I do."

Why'd he ask? I wondered, and then I had to laugh. Why would he have brought a wheelbarrow to an informational meeting? In the thick of winter? It was equal parts freakish and impressive.

He turned on his heel, military-perfect, and strode out. Within seconds, he backed in again, pulling the wheelbarrow through haphazardly, a shovel handle clenched tight in his right armpit. I dashed over and held the doors wide so he could get through unobstructed.

"Thank you, Miss Middlebury," he said. (I wondered whether I took the whole "Miss Middlebury" thing too far. On one hand, the respectfulness of it was appealing. On the other hand, it kind of made me sound like a kindergarten teacher.) He got the wheelbarrow oriented to the room, leaned on the shovel handle, and wiped his brow with a blue bandana he pulled from his back pocket.

"I hate a mess," he said after he'd folded and tucked the bandana away. "Unavoidable on these jobs sometimes, but I hate to start with all this—" he swept an arm across the room, dotted with piles of drywall leavings and sawdust—"littering up the place."

He wheeled over to the first, biggest pile and began shoveling

Robiskey's residue into the wheelbarrow's bucket. When he had a full load, he said, "I'll put it in my truck and take it to the dump today. We'll install a big Dumpster in the parking lot tomorrow. It'll make things easier."

I walked over and took the wooden handles from him.

"You shovel," I said. "I'll cart it out."

He reached for the handles. "My job," he said.

"My gym."

He stepped back, smiling, hands in the air in surrender. "As you wish."

I set my shoulder into the load, not prepared for just how heavy it was, and not willing to let Linus see me struggle. I pushed hard, found my pace, and got it to the double glass doors, which I pushed open and propped with the stoppers. A gale wind barreled into the building.

"Can you handle it if we just leave these doors open?" I asked Linus. "It'll make things easier, despite the cold."

"I can handle that, and so much more," he called back to me, and I had to laugh again.

What an odd guy.

WE WERE AT IT FOR MORE THAN AN HOUR, Linus shoveling the wheelbarrow full, me pushing it up a ramp into the back of his truck and dumping it out, then wheeling it back to him. Despite the chill, we worked up a sweat. His coat eventually came off. I removed my pullover and wrapped it around my waist. It was, simply put, my gym's inaugural workout—legs, glutes, arms, cardio. The whole thing.

"This your first gym?" I asked him.

"You mean, renovating? Yeah."

"What kind of stuff do you mostly do?"

He bent over and picked up some loose wood scraps and tossed them into the bucket. "A lot of bathrooms. That's a smaller investment for most people, and you can really make a dramatic difference by upgrading a bathroom. But I've done some other stuff, too. I redid the kitchen at Sub Commander."

"I love their meatball heroes," I said. Practically drooled it out, to be honest.

"I'm a loyal customer now. Pride in the job, sure," he said. "But I also dig a cheeseburger sub. And their new space is fantastic."

He looked at me after he said it, but not in a way that suggested he was seeking validation. It was deeper, more penetrating. Like he wanted me to absorb it. I looked away and stepped back as he continued filling the bucket.

"You like this better than teaching math?" I asked.

Linus came to a full stop and leaned on the shovel handle, peering at me again with an intensity that unsettled me a bit.

"You really did check up on me," he said.

"You told me to," I said. My back stiffened. I readied myself.

"I'm not complaining. Just observing."

I stepped back another step. "OK."

He considered the ceiling. "I hate popcorn," he said. "So 1970s. I can fix that."

"Huh?"

He looked at me again. "It's an interesting question."

"What is?"

"Teaching math versus being a contractor. I never considered whether I like one more than the other. Isn't that funny?"

"What's funny about it?" I looked up at the ceiling. This linear guy, who'd outlined a back-to-front renovation of my space, couldn't stay on a topic. It gave me whiplash.

"Not *ha-ha* funny, just funny," he said. "I suppose most people consider how much they like something before they do it, but I never did. I loved teaching. I love doing this. It never occurred to me to rate them against each other. I suppose if I'd been permitted to teach the way I wanted to, the way I knew worked, rather than administering standardized tests, I might still be doing it and renovating bathrooms on the weekends."

At once, I flashed on something Rex's brother, a high school English teacher, had said, something almost identical to what Linus had just put out there. Bobby had said he knew how to make reading fun but that the Board of Education was more interested in making kids get a higher aggregate score, which the state and the feds, in their infinite wisdom, had connected to critical school funding. "We're churning out regurgitators rather than thinkers," he'd said. "We're making these kids responsible for crap they shouldn't have to worry about."

As quickly as I'd left, I crashed back into now. "Being your own boss is better than anything else," I said.

"Agreed," Linus replied. "Although you're the boss." He adjusted the shovel in his hands and smiled at me.

"Damn straight," I said. "So get back to shoveling."

He gave me a terse salute and plowed the blade under a pile of sawdust and lifted it into the bucket.

"And, yeah, fix that ceiling," I said.

Linus

Body language

JO-JO'S BODY LANGUAGE DOES MOST OF HER TALKING, although I don't think she realizes it. It's not that I was paying extra attention to Jo-Jo's body—I wasn't, I swear—but I could tell she's someone who's had to hide her feelings, especially her fears, and not give anyone the satisfaction of seeing her suffer.

I saw it when she was wheeling out the debris. She was clearly struggling at first. I could hear her stifled grunts and watched the way she bent her knees so as not to tax her back—good for her knowing proper lifting protocol. She hoisted the wheelbarrow as if it were a barbell twice her bench press maximum, and she pushed it out slowly, forcefully, stubbornly. And I knew that had I dared offered to help, she would have bitten my head off. And maybe she would have been justified. I've learned from working with my students that some will never ask for help because they learned that doing so is a display of weakness. You have to either patiently wait and/or hope for them to come to you when they're in a do-or-die moment, or, if the circumstances are dire, you have to override their refusal and just find a way to help.

It's clear that Jo-Jo is more than capable of taking care of herself. I think if we all have the capacity to do so, we should. But everyone needs a shoulder to lean on now and then.

Yes. I wanted to be her shoulder. But I knew it wasn't going to happen. This was, as Jo-Jo said, a business arrangement. I was OK with that. To put a gym reno on my website could open a lot more doors in terms of small-business contracts. Win-win.

I CAME HOME FROM MIGHTY JO'S GYM JUST AS THE SUN WENT DOWN, which, at this time of year, was around 4:30. Toby met me at the door and butted his head against my ankles, his affectionate hello. I pet the little guy and headed for the kitchen. I placed my phone on the counter, admiring my work on the cabinet doors—all sanded and awaiting paint—and played voicemails on speaker while sifting through what was mostly junk mail.

A familiar voice crackled. *"Hey, it's Amanda."* My stomach lurched. *"About your stuff ..."* Shit. I'd forgotten to follow up on that. *"We need it out of here. So if you could come over and take care of that ASAP, that would be great."*

I bristled. Her tone gnawed at my gut. *It would be great—for her.* I tapped the screen and the phone dialed Amanda's number. I activated the speakerphone and continued to open and shred mail. Amanda picked up on the second ring.

"It's about damn time you called me back," she snapped.

"Hello," I retorted.

"Seriously, Linus, I've been waiting all day."

"I work, you know. And I don't take phone calls while I work."

"Whatever. So when are you coming over?"

I was once in love with this woman. And she with me. It baffled me. How? Had we been deluded? Clueless? How did we get it so wrong? And even though we'd had what I would call an amicable divorce (meaning I caved to her demands in service of getting it over with as quickly as possible), these days we weren't even friends. How do you fall in love with someone you can't even be friends with?

Unless we were never in love. Perhaps it had been nothing more than crossed signals. An infatuation for me; a look-at-the-cute-little-puppy for her. Or perhaps it had been temporary insanity. I don't mean that in a bitter or snarky way. Just that when I look back on it, it seems that neither of us ever really felt grounded. And when we finally were grounded, it came at the expense of a hard thud, a crash-and-burn that left scars.

I could hear words in the huff that rattled like static: *I see you haven't grown a spine yet.*

Thing was, the old me would have dropped everything to retrieve the boxes, just to please her. I was all about trying to please her. And what I learned was that the more I tried to please her, the more she resented me for it, which made me try harder, until it was this vicious tail-chasing circle. I was her puppy. Genial and accommodating and begging for a pat on the head. My therapist had told me I was a rescuer. So did Jennifer. The price to pay for reading too many comic books as a kid, I guess. Or maybe it was hardwired into my DNA.

"I'll come over when I come over," I said.

A pause.

"Really? You're going to be difficult over a bunch of stupid boxes?"

"My stuff is not stupid. And neither is my time. You can't order me around anymore, Amanda. I'll pick them up when it's mutually accommodating."

Another pause.

"Bryce wants to talk to you," Amanda said.

My body stiffened. I hadn't seen or spoken to Bryce since I'd found out about the affair and I went to his office downtown to confront him. I'd taken a swing at him and he'd swerved before socking me in the jaw, sending me somersaulting backward over a chair. When I was able to regain my balance (grateful no ribs were broken), I'd retreated. Said nothing. Did nothing. Just walked out rubbing my jaw. It wasn't a hard punch, but the *humiliation* ... that produced the pain of a thousand punches. I felt like such a *coward*.

Without waiting for my permission, Bryce's voice appeared. "Hey, Linus."

My fists clenched. "Yes?"

"So listen, buddy. Just come pick up your stuff right now and we're all cool, OK? Otherwise we'll have to throw it out."

Buddy.

"The hell you will," I said.

"Come on, man. Why do you have to be such a dick?"

And with that, I tapped the screen and ended the call. Wanted to hurl the phone across the kitchen. Instead I just sat there and steamed. *He* was the dick. So why did *I* feel like one? Why did I burn with the same humiliation as that day in Bryce's office? My hand reflexively went to my jaw.

I glanced at the phone's screen. Larry had left a voicemail as well. I listened: *"Hey, we feel bad about the brouhaha the other morning and want you to meet us at the Brew Pub for dinner tonight. No need to confirm. Just show up if you can. Six-ish."*

I was getting tired of imposing on Larry and Jennifer. It's not like I didn't have any other friends, although one of the suckiest things about divorce is how many friends you lose in the churn. Regardless of whether they do it intentionally, they take sides. And if you're friends with a couple, then sometimes one spouse-friend takes a side and the other goes along. Sometimes they agree to see you on the sly, confessing that they saw things your way. But it's just too damn awkward. Amanda and I had been friends with a lot of couples. I kept Larry and Jennifer. She kept almost all the rest. Par for the course, I guess.

I looked around the kitchen, still in disarray. That was the thing about renovation. You have to do the demolition first. And for a while, everything gets worse before it gets better. You just have to keep your eye on the vision.

Renovation was all about patience. And trust. It was about the endgame.

My stomach growled.

The hell with the endgame.

I put on my coat and texted Larry and Jennifer to let them know I'd be waiting for them at the Brew Pub after I picked up my stuff at Amanda's.

On second thought, I decided to call Amanda and Bryce's bluff. Let them throw my stuff out. I'd lived without it all this time, hadn't I? I was done being a punching bag.

Jo-Jo

It never stops

I HADN'T HAD A GOOD DAY AT MY GYM SINCE THAT DAY IN SEPTEMBER—
the first, as it turned out—when I met the rental agent there and
picked up the key. That was the best day, the tangible arrival of my
dream, the moment that redeemed the crappy sales job I'd worked,
the validation of my insistence on setting aside at least ten percent
of every paycheck, no matter how measly and no matter how much
my bills would stretch whatever was left. I'm talking about nine
long years of struggle, of holding tight to the one dream you've had
even as you've let a million others go, and it comes down to one day.
One day where you write one big check and you get a key. That was
a great day.

Most of them since have been varying shades of disappointing
where the gym is concerned. Waiting a week later than I expected
for the Robiskey pukes to start. Finding out that what I'd budgeted

for renovation was about nineteen percent too skimpy. The stops and the starts and the excuses. That awful morning, right after Thanksgiving, when Dirk Dolan (I'll be saying "fuck you" to that name for the rest of my life) told me they wouldn't be done until late December, and I knew there was no way I'd have a New Year's Day opening (goodbye, social-media campaign!). And then, ten days after that, when Dirk Dolan promised me it would be no later than mid-January and I fired him, right there in the parking lot. He didn't see me cry that day. He's lucky he didn't see my fist plow into his eye.

But today? Today was a good day at my gym.

IF I WERE INTERESTED IN CUTE, I might say Linus Travers was that. We said our goodbyes around four p.m., and he stumbled over his, saying, "Well, this has been … a pleasure, I'd say, and I'm looking forward to getting on with it, I mean the work, not anything else, and, well, have a good evening, Miss Middlebury." I stifled a giggle and offered him a proper handshake, and just for a fleeting second I thought about inviting him out for a beer, but I set that aside. Maybe at the end of this a beer would be appropriate, or nearer the end, anyway. Today, a beer would have carried unintended invitations, and those have a way of becoming uncomfortable situations. I can safely say, now, that I understood why Larry and Jennifer think so much of him. I didn't need to understand anything more than that.

I was two turns from my home in central Billings when the text message popped up, from a number I didn't recognize with a 406 area code.

Jo-Jo, can we talk?

I engaged the voice recognition. "Who's this, question mark." It came out *whose priss?* Dammit, Siri.

Huh? Is that supposed to mean something?

Dammit. That had to be Rex.

Double dammit.

I'd deleted his number the day he left, and I'd never bothered to memorize it before that. Who needs to, when you have a contact list? More important, why hadn't I *blocked* Rex?

"Call me in ten," I said, and I saw after sending that Siri had made it *calm my intention.*

"TEN MINUTES! CALL ME!" I yelled.

Ten minutes call me.

K, he texted back.

I made the final few hundred yards to the carport, white-knuckling it the entire way. The only guy I'd ever given my heart to (actually, I'd given my heart to several guys; Rex was the one I'd thought would keep it)—Big Mistake No. 8,376 by Jo-Jo Middlebury—sure had a way with timing.

"CAN WE TALK?"

I had to give Rex some measure of credit; he could work up a sad-puppy tone of voice when the occasion called for it.

"Yeah, pretty sure we did on New Year's Eve," I said, as I picked up and dropped every piece of mail strewn atop the dining-room table, two of them RSVPs for a wedding that now wouldn't happen. "As I recall, you couldn't commit yourself to a town or a house or a person."

"I—"

"And you see, I'm not a town or a house, but I bear a pretty striking resemblance to a person, so it was hard not to see what you meant by that."

"Jo-Jo—"

"And as I recall, you asked to leave, and I let you, so I ask you, Rex, what is there to talk about?"

"I've been trying—"

"I have plenty of people in my life who are happy to talk about the weather, for example."

"Geezus, Jo-Jo, can you lay off for a minute?"

"For a *whole* minute, or—"

"I deserve this," Rex said. "OK? I deserve it. So I promise you can let me have it if you'll just let me get this one thing out. OK?"

I balled up a fist. And then I felt stupid, and I released it, then balled it up again and punched the back of the nearest chair.

"OK," I said.

"I got scared and I got stupid," he said.

"That's the one thing?"

"Yes."

I stood there, incredulous. "That's it? That's what you came back into my life to tell me, five days after telling me you no longer wanted to be in my life? You think I didn't know this? You think this is some major revelation?"

I could picture him, wherever he was, looking oafish, and I was caught between pity and anger. "I don't know," he replied.

"And what are you expecting me to do with this admission?"

"Take me back, I guess."

I laughed. Hard. Not the kind of laugh from seeing a great comedian or hanging out with your girlfriends and a bottle of wine on a Saturday night. But exasperated, incredulous, I-can't-believe-you-had-the-balls-to-call-me-with-this-bullshit laughter.

"You guess?" I shot back.

I could practically hear his cheeks turning red. "Can you please give me a break, Jo-Jo? This isn't easy for me. I messed up. I know it. Like, really bad. I got cold feet."

Was it really just cold feet? Hadn't he gotten what he wanted by leaving? And hadn't I gotten what I needed, which was a reprieve from a marriage that wouldn't have been any good, no matter how painful his leaving was?

Because, after all, that's what I'd been telling myself for several days now. Better for everybody that this marriage would never happen. It only took me five days to figure that out. Well, five days and the ten months we'd been engaged to be married. Plus the two years we were dating before that.

"I don't think you did," I said. "I mean, I believe that you think you did. But I think it was much more than cold feet."

"Can we at least meet somewhere and talk about it? We've got a lot in the bank, Jo-Jo. A lot of time. Shared experiences. Plans and dreams. If you still think I'm full of shit, then I'm full of shit, and I'll walk away for good. But please, let's talk first."

I closed my eyes. He was right, of course, about the time and the togetherness. Aside from Larry and Caroline the cop, Rex knew more about me than anyone else did. Because I'd let him in, and I'd let him stay. And, yeah, he'd let himself out, and it was for the best, but that didn't mean everything had vanished in less than a week. I still had a heart that felt the absence of what I'd wanted him to be. Of what I'd wanted us to be *together*. But hadn't that heart been squeezed enough? Hadn't it been twisted in knots, ripped out of my chest, broken into pieces over and over again? Why put it through another spin cycle?

I opened my eyes. "When and where?" I hated myself as the words came out. Because, dammit, I still wanted the idea. Not of Rex, but of a mended heart.

He brightened. "How about the Brew Pub at 6:30?" he suggested. "We always had fun at that place."

Mr. Blue Sky

Sometimes, it's just a coincidence. Sometimes ...

HEY, COME OVER HERE. I'm going to do something I've never done before. I'm going to interrupt the first side of the *Saturday Night Fever* soundtrack to share something with you.

Don't look at me like that. First of all, it's freakin' vinyl, man, the only way to listen to it. Second, if you can push yourself beyond your fixation on the fashions—yes, the white polyester suits and big-ass gold chains didn't age well—and focus on the production values, you'll realize that this is one of the great albums of a greatly misunderstood decade. In 2017, *Sgt. Pepper's Lonely Hearts Club Band* turned fifty years old and people couldn't shut up about it. Meanwhile, this album turned forty and it was crickets all around. A damn injustice, that's what it was.

I'm just saying.

Anyway ...

You can see the potential collision we've got here. Just a little while ago, Linus and Larry and Jennifer sat down for dinner at the Brew Pub (it's actually called the Billings Brewing Co., but nobody who lives in Billings calls it that, and who am I to be pedantic on such a minor point?), and soon enough Jo-Jo is going to be coming through that front door, and won't that be interesting?

Maybe. Maybe not.

The lazy-tongued among you, and Alanis Morrissette, might call this ironic. It's not. It's only a coincidence. And it's not even a terribly interesting one. Billings, Montana, is a town on the upswing, and it has some decent restaurants. The Brew Pub is downtown, it's well-established, and it's popular, so the chances that this guy and this woman would be there at the same time are not even remotely remote (see what I did there, Ted Baxter?).

But here's the thing about coincidences: Sometimes, they are isolated collisions. Sometimes, they're the building blocks of a larger narrative that is understood only in hindsight, if it's ever understood at all. That applies to your knowledge and mine, by the way. I don't know what's coming any more than you do. Furthermore, nobody has asked me to get involved, which means I'm putting "Night Fever" back on in about twenty seconds.

But one last thing before you go …

Because my view is more pulled-back than yours, I can see things you can't. For example, I can see that the yellow FJ Cruiser that just turned right onto Broadway is probably going to T-bone that red Volkswagen Beetle turning left onto First Avenue while the former's driver sends a text. My colleague—we'll call him Bob—is responsible for the driver in the VW, so Bob-O has just sounded a *"watch out!"*

I can see something else, too. I can see that Linus just told Jennifer and Larry about his work at Jo-Jo's gym, and I can see that Jo-Jo has her hand on the door handle.

Gotta go now. *There is something goin' down …*

Linus

A guy walks into a bar ...

As USUAL, the Brew Pub was packed, especially on the side of the bar with the high-top tables and wall-to-wall TVs showing basketball games and NFL playoffs commentary and, on one lone screen, a program about fishing. That's the side I was on. The rowdy side. The side without kids. Families were on the other side of a low wall, in sight, but miles away in terms of ambience. Here, you could barely hear yourself think, although in my case that was a welcome plus.

I don't know why I was feeling so sorry for myself. I'd left the gym feeling as if I'd broken ground not only on the project but also with Jo-Jo. Like, maybe, when this was all over, we'd be friends. And not just acquaintances who stopped and said hello if they crossed paths at Albertsons. I mean, one of us could call the other, say something like, "You feel like going to see a movie tonight?" and the other would be like, "Sure. I'll get the tickets if you get the popcorn."

And then we'd meet there and see a movie and maybe have a beer afterward, and that would be that until the next time.

That would be awesome.

Who was I kidding? The call with Amanda and Bryce had put me into a funk. Made me feel like a teenager who'd just refused the joint that all his buddies were passing around, and now they were laughing at him for it. "Come on, don't be such a loser."

No, not a loser. Don't be such a *dick*.

I'd done the right thing by not picking up the boxes, hadn't I? I'd exercised my boundaries, gotten assertive, put myself first. So why did I feel like shit?

Because I'd been too nice. Even in saying no. And I was still coming out the loser. Maybe it wasn't worth anything, but it was still my stuff they were throwing away with the same lack of respect and consideration they'd given Amanda's and my marriage when they began their affair.

Amanda had said this to me once when we'd first started dating. *"You're too nice, Linus."* She'd said it very sweetly, after I'd held the restaurant door open, followed by her chair. A few dates later, when we'd gotten the wrong order of Chinese food and I told the server it was OK, Amanda had said it again, only less admiringly. More like annoyed. "You're too nice, Linus."

And then, when our marriage was being dissolved and I was submitting to almost all of her demands, my lawyer had scolded me, and Amanda said it out loud once more, this time with a smirk of triumph. "You're too nice, Linus." She had used it to her advantage.

My therapist had told me it was a boundary issue. So I'd worked on it. And I'd tried to exercise good boundaries on the phone earlier, because when you finally exercise your boundaries, the people who used to be able to walk all over you can't any longer. And they hate you for it, but you no longer care what they think, because you're free. Also a sign of good boundaries.

I didn't feel free.

This ugly truth hit me at the same time Larry and Jennifer entered the Brew Pub. I caught their faces through two tables full of what I assumed to be office colleagues glued to the Cavs-Celtics game. I rose from my bar stool and flagged them down. They met me, and we walked to the dining area, where we were seated at a booth in front of a family with a five-year-old boy who kept standing on the bench and leaning over to drop Cheetos on me.

"Jeffrey, you cut that out," Jeffrey's mom said.

Oblivious, Jeffrey continued the Cheetos assault.

I turned around. "Hey, Jeffrey, you know what happens when kids don't listen to their moms? Chester the Cheetah comes into your bedroom at night and eats them."

Larry and Jennifer burst into laughter; the water Jenn had taken dribbled out her mouth and down her chin. Jeffrey's face crumpled up in fear as he let out a shriek. And with that, the little monster's mother finally pulled him down, paid the bill, and took him out, fixing me with a nasty stare on her way to the door.

"Seriously, how is this place considered a family restaurant?" I asked.

"Complain to management," Larry said.

"Who'd hear me? It's loud, too. Why do we come here?"

"The food," Jenn said. "And the beer."

Case closed.

As if on cue, the server came and took our orders. (We always ordered the same: a plate of nachos that could feed a family of four for Larry, spicy mac and cheese for Jenn, and a bacon cheeseburger for yours truly. It occurred to me that in addition to being too nice, I was too predictable.)

"So what's up, guys?" I asked.

"The usual," Larry said.

"We just wanted to apologize for the other morning," Jenn said.

I waved her off. "I already told you, it's not necessary."

They nodded, and then I held up my glass and toasted. "No hard feelings." We all clinked glasses and then each took a pull from our beverages in unison, followed by awkward silence save for the gaggle of the patrons and a barely audible Tom Petty song on the sound system.

Larry broke the stalemate. "You start work on Jo-Jo's gym today?" He asked in a way that suggested he already knew the answer.

I grinned. "I sure did," I said. I caught Jenn giving him a scowling side-eye that he either avoided or had evaded him. "It's a big project. But doable. Idiot Robiskey made the job twice as costly, though, both in time and money."

"How did you know he was working on Jo-Jo's gym?" Jennifer asked him.

Uh-oh.

"What do you mean how do I know?" Larry asked.

"Hey, can we not do this again?" I jumped in. "In fact, let's not talk about work. Let's talk football. What do you say to Super Bowl party at my house this year? Living room will be done by then."

I was hoping the more I talked, the further away we'd be from confrontation.

Jennifer shrugged. "Meh. The Patriots are probably going to be in it again. I'm getting a little tired of those assholes."

Larry laughed. *Thank God.*

"There's always commercials," I offered.

"We'll see," Jenn said. She sounded distant.

Larry's phone beeped, and he turned it over. His eyes widened as he lifted his head and scanned the place. Jennifer and I exchanged quizzical looks.

"What's up?" I asked.

"Nothing," Larry said as the server delivered the salads.

"Time to enforce the rule," Jennifer said as she tapped the table.

"Come on. Phones down. First one to pick theirs up also picks up the check."

"I thought you were already picking up the check," I said.

She scowled at me, and I felt the urge to hide under the table. I'd been slow on the uptake yet again.

"New plan," she said.

Larry and I obediently deposited our phones screen down on the table, with Jenn's on top. We both loved a good challenge.

EVEN THOUGH WE KEPT UP THE SMALL TALK AND CRACKED A FEW JOKES, dinner was stilted. Jennifer filled me in on Charlie's math grades, which were up since I'd been tutoring him. It's a side gig I loved, by the way, because the impact was measurable. Bringing math to a kid is just a matter of finding the way he or she is most conversational about it, and Charlie and I had bonded over dinosaurs and galaxies and how those concepts could be explained in numbers.

But even as Jenn and I, and Larry to a lesser degree, babbled about Charlie's soaring scores, it was as if there were an elephant in the room, something or someone we were talking or dancing around. I told them about Amanda's phone call, and both congratulated me for not caving in.

"What's in the boxes?" Jenn asked.

"Probably high school and college memorabilia. My letterman jacket. Mathletes award, some CDs and VHS tapes ..."

Larry looked distracted, unable to keep his eyes on me or his wife. "Like that's worth saving," he finally said, which stung me.

Jennifer scowled again. "That's not the point," she started. "The point is that they don't have the right to boss him around or dispose of his stuff without his permission."

"Fine," Larry said with a huff. "I'm wrong yet again."

I practically cringed, feeling caught in the middle of yet another tug-of-war.

I attempted to play peacekeeper. "It probably is a bunch of junk."

And then, after yet another bout of awkward silence, Larry reached for his phone in the pile and started furiously tapping at it.

"Well, that's that!" I said, in attempt to be cocky, yet playful. "Thanks for dinner, buddy." *Buddy.* I didn't intend it, but my use of the word sounded as patronizing and disingenuous as Bryce's had. Larry wasn't even paying attention.

"You know, you're being extremely rude," Jenn said. She leaned in to get a glimpse at his screen, but he pushed her back to her side of the bench—not hard, mind you, but enough for the two of them to be irked and me to be a massively uncomfortable spectator again. He shoved the phone into his pants pocket, pulled out his wallet, and whipped out a credit card. "We should go," he said, and again as if summoned, the server arrived, processed the payment, and we got up and left.

I was about to lean into the door with my back against it to push it open when I saw what had spooked Larry.

Sitting at one of the pub tables by the window.

Jo-Jo.

And a guy. A going-gray guy in a Steelers jersey.

Her eyes met mine for a second. Registered full recognition for that second, the kind of second that seems way longer, long enough for me to feel like we'd just had an entire conversation. *(Hey, Charlie, how many uncomfortable seconds are in a minute? Six thousand!)* And then she shifted her gaze back to the crew-cutted, jerseyed alpha male sitting across from her.

How do I know he was an alpha male? Because he looked like the kind of guy who'd call another guy a dick.

A shiver coursed through me. And that was before the door to downtown opened and blew in the blast of nighttime winter air.

Jo-Jo

I can only manage me

BEFORE I'D EVEN LEFT MY STREET ON THE WAY DOWNTOWN, my inner voice told me I'd be better off climbing into my jammies, making some mac-and-cheese from a box, and seeing what was on the Turner Classic Movies channel.

I have to learn to listen to that voice. It's smarter than I am.

But I kept driving, because I'd said I would hear Rex out, and I may be many things but I'm not someone who flakes out on her word. (Unlike Rex, I might point out.)

And now a bunch of stuff has happened, and I'm back home, in my jammies, mac-and-cheese-less, and TCM is in the middle of some artsy Japanese movie.

This sucks.

WHAT I'M CONFRONTED WITH NOW ARE THREE DISTINCT ISSUES AND THE people associated with them. For my own clarity, I'll take them one at a time.

Rex: He showed up in a football jersey. At a meeting where his stated purpose was to convince me that he knew he'd made a mistake by blowing up our relationship. Not a good start.

That probably seems nitpicky, fixating on a jersey given the larger questions at hand. And I realize that "judgmental" is probably the adjective most of the people who don't like me—and several who do—use to describe my attitude. But I'm not judgmental. I'm particular. There's a difference. I don't care that Rex likes football, or the Steelers (though I prefer the Seahawks), or even that he likes to wear that jersey, even though I think there's nothing sillier than a man who's twenty years older than a football player and most assuredly not in football shape trying to pull off that look. My point is, had Rex and I been lazing about the house on a Sunday and then decided to go out for a bite and a beer, the jersey is fine. But no. He was at a downtown restaurant, trying to restore his credibility with me. I'd have preferred he dressed his intent.

Linus: I could see it in his eyes. The *what-are-you-doing?* look. The *who-is-that-guy?* look. And I get it. I do. Given the circumstances of how he and I knew each other—that stupid, meaningless, spur-of-the-moment kiss—I understood his bewilderment.

But it wasn't my responsibility to explain it to him. Nor was it his business. I half-expected to hear from him this evening, because in my experience that's what guys do. They demand answers to questions they have no right to ask. But it's been radio silence, and I hope he'll keep his distance Monday, too. He's a good guy doing good work, and I'm going to pay him what's right, so that should be the extent of his interest in me or mine in him. Right?

Larry (and, thus, Jennifer): I texted Larry only because I happened to see him when I came through the door and I was able to imagine—rightly, I might add—the potential for awkwardness should they see me with Rex. I didn't even know Linus was with them, never saw him from my vantage point. I wished Larry could have used the back door to the Brew Pub, instead of hustling Jennifer and Linus out the *front* door, because that's where everything got weird.

They saw me.

I saw them.

Rex saw me see them.

They left.

I stayed.

Rex abruptly shifted the focus of our get-together.

"What's going on there?" he asked, when I got myself turned around and my attention back on him.

"Nothing."

"That guy with Larry was staring at you."

"Really?" I asked. "That's how you want to play this?"

"Jo-Jo, I'm not stupid. The guy was gaping at you. And check this out." Rex pointed out the window, across the empty veranda piled with snow, to the sidewalk, where Jennifer was yelling and poking Larry in the chest, and my old friend was shrinking by the second.

Ouch.

At once, Jennifer turned away from Larry, and he made a grabbing effort to catch her by the arm, whiffing like an overthrown wide receiver. She came back into the restaurant through the front doors and zipped up to our table.

"You need to back off," she said.

I stood up. "No, you need to consider what you're saying." Out of the corner of my eye, I saw Rex slide back in his chair and smirk.

"I'm not scared of you," Jennifer said, though she surely was. A quiver went into her. She didn't need to be. I meant, and mean, her no harm.

"Whatever you think about whatever," I said, "I promise you, it's not."

Jennifer gathered herself. I admired that. Larry stood at the door, bracing himself against it.

"Maybe not," she said. "And yet here we are, with drama, and here you are, in the middle of it."

You know what? That hurt more than it should have, because even though Jennifer's aim was scattered and her target was errant, she'd more or less pinned me. I profess to hate it, but drama finds me.

Larry at last sidled up and took his wife by the elbow. Gingerly. "Let's just go home, Jenn," he said.

She looked down, and then she followed him out. I sat down and looked at Rex, who was still smirking.

"What are you all giddy about?" I asked.

"It's just so typical you."

That did it.

"This isn't going to work out, Rex," I said.

The smirk dissolved and desperation took over. "What if I prove to you that I mean what I say?"

I grew impatient, damn near exhausted. "What do you want from me?"

As if I didn't know. He wanted a do-over. Thought we could just wind the clock back and proceed as if the past week had never happened.

"I want to come home," he said. "I want to show you how serious I am. We can make what happened last week a mirage, a bad dream and nothing more. I know it." He sat up in his chair and set his jaw, as if to say *serious as a heart attack*.

Home. Hah.

"No," I said, and couldn't stop myself from feeling sorry at how quickly he deflated.

"Why?"

"Because it *did* happen. All of it. I wrote to all of our friends, all of the people who love us or you or me, and I told them there would be no wedding. And I did that because you told me you didn't want a wedding, or a marriage, or *me*, and I believed you—"

"So why don't you believe me now?"

I cupped my hands to my face and I leaned in. "Because this doesn't feel honest in the way that did."

His shoulders heaved, and I wished again that he'd worn something else. A button-front shirt. Not Ben Roethlisberger's number.

"So there's just nothing left?" he asked. "I can't accept that. Not after all we've put in together. I'm going to prove to you that I'm being honest."

I reached for his hand, and now, two hours later, I'm still debating whether I should have. "Thing is, Rex," I started. "You shouldn't have to *prove* it."

He pulled his hand away.

I pressed on. "I'm just saying we're in a different place than we were a few weeks ago. I have plans, and your leaving helped put them into clear focus. Those plans, today, right here, right now, don't include going back to what we were."

"After only five days?"

I nodded. "I'm sorry. I told you I'd hear you out, and I have, and this is where I am."

"What if your plans change?" he asked.

"Then they change."

"What if I called you up sometime, and asked you to go to a movie?"

"Rex—"

"No, come on. What if?"

"I guess I'd consider whether I wanted to see a movie with you when you asked."

He leaned in and grinned like a teenage boy. "Do you want to see a movie next week?"

I don't think I even blinked. "No."

That crushed look again. "You're not making this easy," he said.

I waved the server over. "It's not my job to make it easy," I said. I handed her my credit card.

She looked at my plate, and at Rex's. "One bite. Was something wrong with the food?"

"No," I said. "I'm just not hungry."

While she ran the bill, I excused myself to go to the restroom.

When I got back, Rex was gone. He stiffed me with his bill, too.

Replaying it all now, I think I handled it correctly. At the very least, I did the best I could.

So why do I have this dread in the pit of my stomach?

Linus

Get back in the game

The house was dark, lit only by the streetlamps and motion sensor lights casting shadows on the walls through the windows. I sat at the computer desk in what was going to be my office—the smallest bedroom of the three—and I stared at the screen, squinting as I read what I'd just typed:

If you think reading is sexy, I'll bring you a book.
If you think cooking is a contact sport, I'll apron up.
If you think Cary Grant and Audrey Hepburn had great chemistry, I'll wear a drip-dry suit.
If you like sports but dislike sports fans, I'll turn down the sound.
Call me old-fashioned, but I think building a relationship requires more than a swipe-right/swipe-left

decision. It requires mutual respect. Trust. A sense of humor. Most of all, it requires friendship. A conversation. One milkshake with two straws.
  Would you like to share?

I wanted to be genuine and charming. Cute, yet concise. But there's no way to write a dating profile that isn't just a little bit dishonest. I wouldn't call it outright lying, but in trying to make a winning first impression, you leave so much out. Like being divorced. And lonely. And living in a house that looks like a contractor's nightmare rather than a showplace. There's no way to write that you feel caught in the middle of your two best friends, who are clearly having some sort of problem, and knowing you can't help because it's none of your business.

Most of all, you can't write that the whole reason you're doing this is that a woman, for reasons unknown, happened to find you in room full of possibilities and planted a random kiss on you—and perhaps it was a spell. And now she has made it clear that any notions you had about fate are moot.

Dinner at the Brew Pub with Larry and Jennifer had been awkward enough. So was that moment upon exiting when everything except Jo-Jo and me came to a halt. It was like catching the football only to be pummeled by a linebacker—in a Steelers jersey—a yard short of a first down.

You have no idea how much I wished it didn't bother me that she was there with a guy, especially after Jennifer told me who he was. She'd texted me shortly after I'd gotten home: *Can I call you?*

Seconds after I replied with a thumbs-up emoji, Jennifer's photo appeared on my buzzing phone screen, and I tapped it. "What's wrong, Jenn?"

She sniffled. "I think Larry and I are in trouble."

Shit. I thought so, too, but I hoped not.

I settled in on my bed, not bothering to turn on a light. "What happened? You both seemed fine at the party. And before then."

"We've been hiding it pretty well up until ... I don't know, lately it's like he's not here," she said. "Even when he's in the room. *Especially* when he's in the room. And I don't know what's wrong because he's not talking to me, even to complain. Heck, at this point I'd prefer it if he complained. At least then I'd know."

There's a song by Duran Duran called "You Kill Me With Silence." (Yes. I'm a heterosexual male who likes Duran Duran. And yes, they're still around. They still write their own songs and play their own instruments. And they wear scarves. I don't know any guy over fifty who can wear a pink scarf and still look studly the way they can.) It's about a woman who uses silence as a weapon in her relationships. Perhaps the most chilling lyric refers to it as "emotional violence." I related to it more than I wanted to admit to anyone, even myself. By the end of our marriage, Amanda and I used silence as a survival tactic rather than as a weapon.

The song popped into my head and started playing on repeat. Especially the chorus.

"How long as this been going on?" I asked.

"Too long," Jenn said. Why hadn't she said anything sooner? Or maybe she'd tried, and I was too wrapped up in my own post-marital woes to notice.

"For what it's worth, he's not said a word to me about it," I offered. "Maybe it's just some stress that has nothing to do with you. Maybe it's a midlife crisis."

I instantly regretted that last suggestion; the last thing Jenn needed to worry about was Larry coming home having traded in his Subaru for a Harley-Davidson and announcing that he was quitting his job and taking a road trip across America with a gang of other forty-something white guys. Besides, given that he was in media marketing, it would've been massively cliché. Not to mention that he didn't even like driving the mountain pass between Bozeman and Livingston.

"And of course, there's all this drama with Jo-Jo," Jenn said, having seemingly not heard anything I'd just said.

I braced myself. "What do you mean?"

"I always felt a little more secure when she was in a relationship— not much, mind you, but at least then she didn't run to Larry every five seconds, and Larry didn't feel the need to rescue her. A relationship kept her at bay, I guess."

I sat up and re-propped the pillows against the headboard. "You really think he's trying to rescue her? Because you both made it very clear that she doesn't go for that sort of thing."

"Jo-Jo Middlebury is like a tornado; she just sucks everyone and everything into her wind funnel and then spits them out somewhere else when she's done storming. Regardless of whether she's doing it intentionally, that's what happens. And Larry ... well, Larry's like one of those guys who go chasing the tornado for the thrill of it."

That didn't sound like Larry at all. He was practical. Grounded. Solid. Was Jo-Jo Middlebury some kind of spellbinder?

"Why?" I asked.

"Jo-Jo dumped *him*, not the other way around," she said. "I think he's been trying to figure out why ever since. Or at least trying to make her admit that she'd made a mistake."

My mind reeled. I hadn't figured on a Larry's-still-got-unresolved-feelings-for-Jo-Jo dynamic. And I suddenly felt jealous of, angry at, and sorry for him all at the same time.

But this was about my friend, the mother hen who'd helped me through the worst period of my life. I needed to mother her. "Jenn, Larry loves you. I can see it every time he looks at you."

Jennifer sobbed. "Larry loves the fact that I love him in spite of everything."

"What do you mean, in spite of everything?" I asked. "I really don't understand."

"Of course you don't," she said. "Because you're conscientious and considerate of others. You do the dishes and take out the garbage in other people's houses. You clean up other people's messes. You see the potential that lives between the flaws in every person you meet. You shape young minds."

Her compliments made my heart swell. It had been a long time since I'd heard outright admiration, and I realized I missed it. Needed it. But her words also made my cheeks flush. I was tempted to ask if she had me confused with someone else.

"Do you know who Jo-Jo was with tonight?" she asked.

I shook my head as if Jenn and I were face to face. "No."

"Rex. Her fiancé who allegedly dumped her."

And just like that, I lurched as if I'd just been sucker-punched. *"What?"*

"You heard me."

"How—" The words stuck in my throat.

"Jo-Jo had texted Larry that she was there with him. I swear, this whole thing has been a ruse just so she could get everyone's sympathy."

I didn't want to pile on Jenn, but I just couldn't swallow that about Jo-Jo. Drama is one thing. Fabricating a canceled wedding (or getting engaged just so you could cancel it to garner attention) seemed incongruent with her. "You really think she'd go through all that trouble and expense of canceling a wedding just to get a few extra hugs?"

"She probably never canceled it in the first place. Rex probably just went hunting for a few days. I told you, Linus. She's a tornado."

Was I being naïve to want to think the best of Jo-Jo or to be so quick to stress-test Jenn's theories? Was I betraying my friend by doing so? And why was Jenn suddenly aggressively anti-Jo-Jo after being so matter-of-fact and basically complimentary when we first talked about her on New Year's Day?

And even if Jenn was wrong, it didn't change the fact that, if nothing else, Jo-Jo and her questionable ex had some unfinished business. Or that reconciliation was possible. I felt as if I'd been pummeled yet again. The same as when I'd found out that Amanda was cheating on me with Bryce.

You'd think Jennifer had just read my mind. "Linus, I have a confession."

Oh, God. I don't think I can take it.

"What is it?" I asked. My voice cracked.

"When I saw the way you looked at Jo-Jo and Rex tonight ... I don't know ... something in me snapped. It's bad enough Larry never got over her, but *you* ..."

Was that true? Had Larry never gotten over her? Was *that* the reason he'd steered me away from pursuing Jo-Jo, and not her state of mind following her would-be ex-fiancé dumping her? And was Jennifer telling me she was jealous of Jo-Jo because of me rather than because of Larry?

"Jenn, I'm not—"

"Just please, please forget all about Jo-Jo. You'll be glad later."

"I have," I said. "I mean, as a romantic prospect. I told you that. But I'm not going to give her up as a client. I gave her my word, and I need the work. The guys I hired need the work, too."

"You should be with someone who loves and appreciates you just as you are."

She wasn't wrong about that. I'd been coming to that conclusion for a year now.

Nothing had changed since New Year's Eve, before that damn kiss. I was tired of being alone. I was tired of waiting. I was tired of being everyone's buddy. If anything, the absence of a lover, someone warm and soft and twinkling, had expanded from a gaping hole to a bottomless crater.

It was time to do something about it.

Put another way: when you get tackled that hard, you sit out a few plays, and you get back in the game. You play hurt, but you play.

So that's what I'd decided to do.

I should have done it a long time ago. I certainly should have done it before New Year's Eve.

Or maybe I should have protected my heart.

"You're right," I said. "Thanks, Jenn."

She didn't say anything else.

"Do you want me to talk to Larry?" I asked.

She stammered for a second before answering. "I guess so."

"I'll sound him out. I'm sure he's just stressed out about work or something. You and Charlie are the best things in his life. He knows it. I know he knows it. And if I have to, I'll remind him of it."

Jennifer abruptly replied, "I have to go," and the call cut out. I wondered if Larry had just walked in the room. Or maybe Charlie did.

I shuddered.

And that's when I went to the computer desk, signed up at PlentyofFish (for starters), and pieced together a dating profile.

I copied and pasted the same description on three dating sites, uploaded my faculty ID photo (hey, it's a good photo, even if it is two years old), used the handle @Linus, and activated each profile.

I was officially back in the game. And within ten minutes, I had a notification:

I like Linus, too. Can I be your Lucy?

Mr. Blue Sky

It's up to you to do the ha-cha-cha

REMEMBER THE MOVIE *Oh God!*? It came out in 1977. George Burns as God. John Denver as the straight man (God's chosen messenger). Larry Gelbart wrote it. Carl Reiner directed it. (Rob Reiner's father. Who's Rob Reiner, you ask? Don't you know "Meathead," meathead? And the director of *The Princess Bride*? You guys have to watch more Hulu.) Lots of comedic talent there. It's a cute little movie that became a smash hit and made an 81-year-old man one of the hottest stars in the world. And the country-folk singer wasn't doing too badly, either.

Anyway, while much of it was playful, there's something in particular I believe they got right, and that was God's message for Jerry Landers to deliver: *I gave you everything you need. It's up to you to make it work.*

This isn't religious dogma, and if you do or don't believe in a

God, that's fine. I'm not here to offer an opinion on that one. Let's not even get universal. Let's talk strictly in terms of your world. Everything was designed, formed, evolved—describe it any way you want—to allow you to support each other. Trees and humans support each other. Water and land support each other. The sun supports plants. The plants support animals. And so on. You have resources and technology to provide yourselves and others with basic needs: food, clothing, and shelter. Plus things to keep you content, like Solitaire on your desktop computer. Most of all, you don't only have everything you need to take care of yourselves. You have everything you need to *take care of each other*.

You were hardwired to do it, in fact. So then why are there so many homeless and hungry? Why so many murders and assaults? Why all the wars? I'm oversimplifying this explanation, I admit, but here's one idea: Because somewhere along the way, phrases like "every man for himself" and "survival of the fittest" and "individualism" took over the conversation. Moreover, you were hardwired to accept or reject those maxims. To follow them or lead by a different example.

Which superhero first used the line "With great power comes great responsibility"? I'm not up on my Marvel or DC. (I'm more of a *Greatest American Hero* type.) But I think we can all agree that the key there is your freedom to accept or reject the responsibility. You can take care of only yourself, or take care of each other. You can take care only of your stock portfolio, or you can take care of your planet. And for the record, I'm not suggesting being rich is evil. Something always comes to one at the expense of another, regardless of what that something is. But again—how do you *respond* to that?

Here's how this applies to Jo-Jo and Linus. Jo-Jo, through no fault of her own, adopted that I'm-beholden-only-to-me philosophy because that's what was shown to her. Time and again, she was put in situations in which no one took responsibility. No one cared for her. Thus, when she says, "It's not my problem," she's protecting her way of life. If she lets someone in—Rex, Larry, the waitress who expressed concern over the untouched food—then they might withdraw that care as quickly as they offered it. She's afraid to *want* someone to take care of her, much less *allow* it. What she doesn't realize is that the thing she fears so deeply *has already happened*. It doesn't have to happen again. She can choose something else.

However, Jo-Jo also has yet to realize that she gets a payoff from the drama she attracts. Drama forces her to go into survival mode. If she has no drama, and she's not in survival mode, then will she actually survive? For Jo-Jo, that is the most terrifying thought of all.

As for Linus, he's realizing that responsibility also comes with boundaries. He can't get sick enough to help someone else who's sick. He can't get poor enough to help someone else who's poor. What he's realizing is what the flight attendants say during the pre-flight safety instruction: You need to put on your own oxygen mask *before* you help someone else put on hers. He's learning how to do that. He took a bold move by joining those dating sites. He's leaving his comfort zone. His reasons for having done so might be questionable, but he's learning as he goes. And time will tell if he did the right thing.

You have to want to make change. And you have to love yourself before you can give or receive love. You have everything you need to make your world a better place for yourselves and others. *If* you want to. Whatever your belief about how your world came to be, you've been given the tools. What nobody can give you is the want-to.

As the great Jack Gilford playing Mr. Foreman in *Enter Laughing* says: "Everything is *if*. It's up to you, *if* you want to do the ha-cha-cha."

What? You don't know that one, either? 1967, man. Also directed by Carl Reiner. You need to look it up. And watch it. Seriously. What kind of guardian angel would I be if I didn't at least point you in the direction of good comedy?

Jo-Jo

It's a matter of endurance

LINUS TRAVERS KICKED ME OUT OF MY GYM.

OK, let me be fair: He asked me to leave, politely, and I listened to his reasons for the request and I left.

It was only later that I began to think of it as being kicked out, and now, yeah, I'm pretty sure that's what happened, no matter how courteous he was about it. And it's been a few hours now, and I still don't know how to feel about it. Angry? Bewildered? Powerless?

All of the above.

We were out of sorts from the time we greeted each other.

"Hey, Linus," I said. "Here we go."

"Morning, Miss Middlebury," he said.

I offered him a cup of coffee—I'd swung by the City Brew on Grand on the way—but he patted his coat pocket and said, "Got a thermos. Thanks, though."

"Well, come on in," I said, turning for the door.

"My flooring guy will be here soon," he said. "I'll just wait in the truck."

"That's silly."

"No, really, it's fine. Can't do much until Carl gets here anyway."

"Um, OK." I went inside. It was one of those bone-cold January days, clear and flat-out frigid. *Let him freeze in the truck if that's what he wants*, I figured.

Inside, I paced around the place. Linus had brought more order to it than I thought possible after so little time on the job. The flooring materials—industrial carpet for the high-traffic walking areas, rubber matting for the equipment pods, and a high-grade synthetic for the running track that would ring the interior—were laid out for easy access in the order Linus would need them. Once the flooring was down, he said, I could better visualize what everything would look like once the equipment was in place. I looked forward to that day. For the first time in I don't know how long, I felt like Mighty Jo.

At once, I wished he'd come inside so I could tell him that. So I could thank him for letting me feel like this was all going to work. I'm not used to sweeps of optimism. I find it easier to expect and prepare for a letdown. If something comes through, great. My expectations are exceeded. If it doesn't, I'm spared the feeling of loss. Cynical? Maybe. I like to think of it as pragmatic. I could give you no fewer than five hundred examples from my own life where pragmatism was the smarter play.

I looked out the big front window at Linus. He had his face down, intent on his phone, as he pecked away at the keys.

"This is stupid," I said aloud. Too loud. I'd taken two steps toward the door, to go outside and tell him, "Look, come inside and let's talk about last night." That's what this was about, right? We'd had this weird moment, and maybe we should just get it on the table.

As I pushed open the door and stepped through and Linus looked up from his phone at me, Carl's truck rolled up. Seconds later—truly, it was just seconds, as neither Carl nor Linus was completely out of his vehicle—a van from Magic City Florist pulled up in front of the curb where I now stood.

The van driver's head popped out of the window. "Jo-Jo Middlebury?"

"Yeah," I said.

"Got something for you."

She came out of the driver's side door and scurried around to the other side, where she rolled back the door, reached in, and pulled out a vase filled with red roses.

I looked at her, then to the offered flowers, then to my left at Linus and Carl, who regarded the scene the way you might look at your refrigerator if it started talking to you.

I took the flowers.

"Somebody sure likes you," the delivery woman said.

"Thanks."

"Come on, Carl," Linus said. "We've got a lot to do today."

Not five minutes later, I got kicked out of my gym.

OK, so I'm probably being dramatic with the whole "kicked out" thing. But it's undeniable that things between me and Linus went from weird to polite and terse after the flowers showed up.

I followed the guys in while fumbling with the card tucked into the roses. Not that I didn't know who was behind them.

I'm not going anywhere, Jo-Jo. I love you. Rex

I had to wonder if it was a threat or a promise. I thought I'd held my ground with Rex, but maybe I'd also given him some threadbare hope that he could find his way back. Now here's real, honest-to-goodness cynicism: I figured I'd have to endure a few of these overtures, until Rex satisfied himself that he'd given it a try, and then he'd be on his way, blaming me. *I gave her a chance*, he'd tell his buddies, *so what more can I do?* And then that would be that. Geez, what was wrong with me? Why was this seemingly OK with me? Why was I actually expecting it?

Because it was all part of the dysfunction, I suddenly realized. It's not that drama followed me wherever I went as if it were a lost puppy. No, I *created* the circumstances for it. I was actually more comfortable spinning in that chaos because I understood it.

That realization, although enlightening, was also depressing, because I didn't know how to undo chaos. Rather, I didn't know who to be, or how to be, in the absence of it.

I set the vase down on the floor in front of the big window and the morning light streaming through.

"Miss Middlebury," Linus said, "I'd rather you didn't leave them there. We're going to be all over this place today, and they'll just get in the way."

I picked it up again and tried to set it on the windowsill. The base was too wide.

"There's not really anywhere else," I said.

"Maybe just take them home," Linus said.

"OK."

"In fact," he added, "it'll probably be best if you just let us work. Things are going get messy today, and we don't want to inconvenience you."

"It sounds like *I'm* the inconvenience."

Linus smiled thinly. "Either way, Miss Middlebury."

"OK."

"I'm sure you have lots of other stuff to do," he said.

Yeah. I can go home and wonder what the hell is wrong with every man on the planet. A second thought retorted sarcastically, *Right. It's the men who have problems. Not you.*

"Shut up," I muttered under my breath.

I gathered up my duffel bag and the flowers, and I left.

Two blocks away, as I sat at the light at Eighth and Grand, I punched the steering wheel.

WHEN I GOT TO THE HOUSE, I launched myself into a cleaning frenzy. Wedding invitation responses, opened and unopened, got shredded. Paid bills, credit-card solicitations, unread magazines, cooking spices I didn't use or had never opened, all of it got ripped apart, thrown away, dispensed with, moved out of my orbit. By cleaning my home, maybe I could simultaneously clean the past, clean every mistake I'd ever made, and every flaw I've ever had. Maybe I could clean the chaos so that it wouldn't be so inviting or familiar anymore. Maybe I could just completely wash away Jo-Jo Middlebury as she previously existed and start over with ... well, a clean slate.

I was halfway finished with vacuuming the living room when my phone vibrated against my hip.

Sorry about Friday night.

I shut the vacuum cleaner off. *WTFF, Larry?* I spelled out with my thumbs in record time.

I was going to ask you the same thing, he replied.

It's not what it seems. Statement of the century. How lame.

One-word response from him: *Good.*

I was hoping he'd leave it at that when he texted again. *Can we meet up?*

I shook my head as if he could see me. *Not a good day.*

I need to. Really.

Dammit.

Every fiber in my being knew what two letters I needed to type. The voices in my head were screaming at me. Even Cholly was looking at me like, *"You know better, dipshit."*

OK, I tapped, along with the send button.

Wrong. Two. Letters.

I could almost hear him sigh in relief, while Cholly looked at me with utter disappointment.

The usual?

Fine, I typed. *10-15 mins.*

Cool.

I left the vacuum cleaner where it stood, gathered my keys and my coat, and headed for the door. As I passed by the kitchen table, I scooped up Rex's red roses and dropped them in the garbage can.

So much for cleaning out the chaos.

Linus

Stacked

I have a date tonight. And I don't mind telling you I'm pretty stoked about it.

I texted Jenn those words just as my phone pinged from—you guessed it—my date. Sari. Who may have dictated her message to Siri. I amuse myself.

SPOILER ALERT: I will be wearing shoes.

I chuckled. Sari was funny. The older I get, the more this is an important quality in any woman I am friends with or dating. Especially dating. When Amanda and I first started dating, I'd found her funny in a sarcastic way. The more I got to know her, however, the more I came to see that it wasn't humor but snark. And sometimes it was very pointed snark. And sometimes that snark was pointed at me. At my expense. Disguised as love. That's how she gaslighted me.

"Oh, Linus," she'd say. "It's a love tap. Don't you know a love tap when you see one?"

Some of the emotional bruises from those love taps lasted for days.

So far Sari and I have only texted. But we almost immediately established a witty back-and-forth, and by this morning I knew I wanted to meet her for dinner.

And not that I want to be one of those guys who judge solely on appearance, but she wasn't bad-looking, either. Smoky eyes. Hair dyed the color of cabernet. Lipstick to match. I wondered if she hung out with the goths when she was in high school.

So we sealed the deal (for dinner!) earlier, around the same time a bouquet of roses arrived at the gym for Jo-Jo, and I'd been looking forward to it ever since.

Speaking of Jo-Jo ...

I was proud of myself for maintaining my boundaries and being professional. Didn't talk about what I'd seen at the Brew Pub on Friday. Didn't say one word about the flowers, which I'd be willing to bet came from the fiancé and weren't any of my business anyway. My business was the gym, and I was pleased with the amount of progress we'd already made. She's going to have locker rooms by the beginning of next week. That's huge.

My one misstep might have been when I asked Jo-Jo to leave—I think she took offense—but I was honestly trying to assure her that her gym was in good hands. And I wanted to protect her flowers. Someone obviously went through the trouble. Would have been a shame for them to have been covered in sawdust or drywall dust or anything else that was floating around as we drilled, nailed, and screwed the place (no, I am *not* being euphemistic). It's going to be a beautiful space when it's done. It's going to be efficient. Snazzy. It's going to kick ass.

For the first time since New Year's Eve, I felt good. At peace.

Because I'd noticed something with Jo-Jo. She wasn't funny. At least not in the way I'd originally thought. And she's obviously not available.

I replied to Sari: *In that case, you leave me no choice but to wear pants.*

She immediately pinged back with a laughing emoji.

Jennifer didn't reply.

But Larry did. Called me, that is. "Hey, man, can we grab a beer?"

"Can't," I replied. "I have a date." I broke into a goofy grin. It felt so good to say it. It felt so good to *have* it.

"Who with?" He sounded taken aback. Suspicious. Defensive, even.

"Her name is Sari. I jumped into the pool, man. It was way past time."

He paused for a beat. "Oh. OK. Well, maybe later this week."

"Everything OK, Lar?"

"It's fine."

Biggest lie ever.

"OK, then." I didn't really know what else to say. Neither did he, and an awkward pause took over. Larry put a stop to it and rushed off the phone.

I didn't remember experiencing awkwardness with Larry before.

SARI AND I HAD ARRANGED TO MEET AT STACKED AT 6:30—we'd had five minutes of banter just on the restaurant's name—and she entered right on time, just as I'd been seated at a table halfway down the long corridor that formed the bulk of the space. Her hair color made her instantly recognizable, and she'd styled it up like Audrey Hepburn's. The rest of her was adorned in a long orange sweater over black leggings and high-heeled pumps. A colorful lime necklace, bracelet, and earring set capped it off. She looked like a tree in the pique of autumn. I mean that as a compliment. Her sweater accentuated her body type. She looked great. And her smile was the main attraction.

I stood up as she approached me in recognition, but still she asked "Linus?" just to make sure. I extended my hand. "Hey!" She took it, but almost seemed disappointed. Had I just committed a *faux pas*? Was I supposed to have kissed her on the cheek? Given her a hug?

I've been out of the game a long time.

I asked if she wanted the chair side of the table or the booth side. "Chair," she replied. "I hate sliding in and out of those things." I pulled what had been my chair out for her, helped her get seated, and then slid behind the table on the bench.

"You look pretty," I said.

She beamed. "Thanks."

"Correction. You *are* pretty."

She beamed brighter. "Why, thank you, kind sir."

I peered at the side of the table. "Nice shoes."

She laughed, and did the same. "Nice pants."

I laughed.

And then … silence. *Shit, already?*

Luckily, a server came to take drink orders, and Sari picked up her menu after he left.

"I always want to get ordering out of the way before conversation," she said. "First things first."

"I agree," I said, although truth be told, I didn't have an opinion either way.

I don't know much time actually passed before the server returned with drinks, but it felt as if we'd sat there, staring at our menus for some time, saying little. I had attempted to incorporate a little bit of talk by commenting on some of the menu items I'd had in the past, but she did nothing more than nod the way you do when you hear someone speaking but aren't listening to a word they're saying. I feared it was going to be like this throughout dinner.

We ordered. And when the server left, Sari put both hands on the table, sat up straight, and said, "Well, Linus. What should we talk about first?"

I exhaled and smiled. *Hooray!*

"I don't know," I said. "Have you dated a lot since joining the site?"

"A little bit," she said. "I've only been on for about six months."

"You're my first," I said, and quickly added, "date, I mean. Your message arrived within minutes of my posting the profile."

"I noticed that," she said, and giggled. "I'm honored to pop that cherry. So you're divorced, I take it?"

I nodded. "A little over a year. I wanted a grace period before I got back in. You know, to make sure I was ready."

"That's smart," she said. "I think too many men—and women, too—jump in way too soon. Like, a guy barely moves out of the house and he's already on Tinder. What's up with that?"

"Oh, Tinder freaks me the hell out."

She laughed and high-fived me before moving on to the next topic. "So tell me what you do."

I told her about the contracting and the teaching school before it. And she told me all about being an occupational therapist. The conversation, even though somewhat contrived with those getting-to-know-you prompts, managed to flow comfortably. Sentence by sentence, we collected data. Similar tastes in food and sports. Completely different tastes in music and movies. A little mix and match for television. As far as home went, she'd only ever known Billings. I had spent my college years in Fort Collins, and even taught my first year of school there.

"So what made you move back to Billings?" she asked.

"I guess I thought it needed me more than Denver did."

"That's sweet," she said.

We continued to talk after our entrées arrived. Best dates. Worst dates. Best place to get a hamburger in Billings. Worst place to get a hangover. And so on. Sari had a son about Charlie's age. Same school, too. I asked her if the boys knew each other. She shook her head. "Doesn't ring a bell."

"So tell me your biggest heartbreak," she said.

I stiffened. And to my surprise, it wasn't Amanda who popped into my head, but Jo-Jo. "I'd rather not," I said.

Her brow furrowed, as if I'd waved a red flag. "Is the wound still fresh?"

"No," I said, unsure of whether I was being truthful. "I'm not even sure it's a wound, to be honest. I'd just rather not dwell on past relationships."

"We discussed best and worst dates. How is this different unless you're still not over it?"

"Point taken. It was my marriage. And believe me, I'm completely over it. But divorce sucks."

Yes, I'd dropped a lie. But it was the only way to get over the bump.

"Damn straight. OK, so what do you want from a relationship, Linus?"

I paused to collect my thoughts. "A lot of what I said in my profile. I want someone to share the little things in life with. Reading books. Cooking a meal. Watching a movie at the Art House. Catching a Mustangs game once summer finally arrives. Most of all, I want someone I can *talk* to, and laugh with. I want a friend."

"Just a friend?"

"Well, yeah. I mean, not only a friend, but I want that to be the foundation."

She seemed to process this, and not necessarily in a *how nice* way, but rather, *well, that's a little weird.*

"Have you been with many women, Linus?"

I shrugged. "A few. How about you?"

"I haven't been with any women."

I laughed. "I meant—"

She smiled. "I know what you meant. I dated a lot all throughout college. And it's not that I married the first man I met after I graduated, but I knew the minute we said 'I do' that I'd made a huge mistake. But I talked myself out of it, you know? It's easier to fool yourself into thinking you can fix it than admit to the huge mistake, and the embarrassment of it."

I nodded. With me, I had been in such denial with Amanda I didn't even realize I'd made a mistake until we were a good two years in. And then it became exactly like Sari said.

"What do you want, Sari?" I asked.

"I want to have a good time. For now, anyway." *Quick answer.*

"Have you had a good time with me so far?"

She smiled, and her eyes sparkled. They were lovely. "Definitely."

I smiled back at her. "Me, too."

"You're cute." Her tone was more flirtatious this time.

"Am I?"

She nodded slyly. "What's your sex policy?"

I straightened my posture. "My sex policy?"

"How many dates before you'll have sex?"

"Oh," I said, and fidgeted with my silverware. "I've never done it on the first date, if that's what you're asking."

"Old-fashioned?" she asked.

"I don't think so. It just doesn't jibe with what I want."

"Friends," she said.

"Friends *first*."

"OK," she said. "I'll try it your way."

My way? Had she been planning to go to bed with me after dinner? I was almost disappointed that I'd just taken that option off the table. And then, in the next moment, relief flooded in. I wasn't ready for that.

Neither of us had dessert. I paid the check, we walked down to the corner of Broadway and Fourth, and she pointed down the street to where she was parked.

"Want me to walk you there?" I asked.

She shook her head. "I'm good. But I would like a kiss, though. That is, if you don't mind kissing a friend."

She was only a couple of inches shorter than me. I tilted my head down to meet her lips, puckered, and touched, letting them linger. She smelled like flowers. And steak.

It was a nice kiss.

"Goodnight, Linus."

"Goodnight." I couldn't feel the ground under my feet.

"Will you call me tomorrow?" she asked.

"I sure will."

"Good." And with that she headed toward her car. I watched her, and when she was out of eyeshot and I turned around to find my own car, for a split second I could have sworn I saw Jennifer, watching me from across the street. But when I did a double-take, she was gone. If she was ever there.

Jo-Jo

This also isn't my problem. Then again ...

I NEARLY HIT LARRY WITH THE DOOR WHEN I ENTERED CITY BREW. That
was the first hint that something was wrong with him, or maybe
the second after the edgy set of text messages. Good old easygoing
Larry would have been at one of the high-top tables, lost in his
phone, and I'd have had to drag him into the present.

This guy at the door, on the other hand, was twitchy, impatient.
"You're late," he said, turning and leaving me there in the entryway.

I followed him, my irritation already on a half-boil. "Like, two
minutes."

"Sit down," he said. He motioned at the opposite seat, then
swept his arm across the tabletop, clearing a few rogue crumbs, and
placed a latte in front of me.

"What's your deal?" I asked, sitting.

"What's yours?" he came back at me, fierce and aggressive, as if he was pre-empting me. You know, the best defense being a good offense, and all of that.

I stood as quickly as I'd sat. "No time for this, Larry. See ya."

He reached across the table—lunged, to be honest—and caught my wrist in his hand. "Please don't."

I sat again, after I shook loose his hold. Anybody else, and I'd have cut that hand off. I looked left and right to make sure no one was paying attention.

"Let's start again, OK?" I said. "At the beginning, like I'm a person worthy of your consideration and respect, because I am."

"I'm sorry." And that was that, as if the whole stormy beginning had been occupied by some Larry I didn't know or recognize, and wouldn't have chosen for a friend. He came back to me. The person I could talk to about anything, who knew my past and what I wanted for my future. I'd never been so thrilled for anyone when he met and fell in love with Jennifer, nor had I ever been so envious of the life they'd been building together since.

That, as it turned out, was the source of his struggle.

"I think Jenn and I are on the outs," he said, and I about spilled the latte before it even reached my lips.

I dropped my jaw. "Since when?"

"Seems like it happened overnight, but I guess it's like gaining weight. You don't notice it until one day nothing fits."

"Are you sure?"

"I don't know. Maybe. It's not good, that much I know."

"Talk to me."

He shifted his weight back and forth on his seat. He clasped his hands. His knuckles formed white ridges beneath the skin.

"Well, you were there," he said, his allusion clear.

"Yes. Yes, I was," I said as the events at the Brew Pub fast-forwarded in front of my mind's eye like those weather alerts on TV.

"So anyway," he said, "we argued all the way home. I told her she was out of line to go after you that way, and, man, everything came out sideways."

"What do you mean, everything? What's everything?"

"She said it wasn't you, but my attitude toward you, and that she didn't want you corrupting—that was her word, *corrupting*—Linus the way you had me."

"Linus? I was there with Rex. What does Linus have to do with anything?"

"That's exactly what I asked her, along with what she meant by corrupting, but she just kept going off. Linus this, Linus that, Linus is so good, on and on."

"Geezus."

"So, finally," he said, "I say to her, 'Jenn, it sounds like you don't think much of me.' And she said, 'I don't. Not like I used to.'"

"*Geezus.*"

"Yeah," he said. "So I slept downstairs on the couch. Left this morning before she and Charlie were awake." He looked at me, plaintively, his eyes red and shot through with a lack of sleep.

I suddenly wondered how different the world would be had I just simply decided not to go to the Brew Pub. It's mind-boggling how one little choice has such a ripple effect. And not that this was all about me, or that I have some tremendous power, but think about it: would things be weird between me and Linus right now? Would Larry and Jenn be OK? Would Rex still think we had a chance?

The heartache I felt on Larry's behalf came in a rush, as well as the need to help him find some hope.

"I bet when you go home tonight, she'll apologize," I said. "That doesn't sound like Jenn. I mean, I don't know her that well, but it seems unusual."

"Maybe," he said.

I braved a smile for him. Behind it, my own mental wheels were spinning. I think I could have dealt with this more easily if I could fixate on what, exactly, Jenn's problem with me was. I've always tried to be sensitive to what she might feel about my friendship with Larry—I mean, ex-lovers-turned-buddies is pretty uncommon. And I've always gotten the vibe from her that she was OK with our friendship, if not enthusiastic about it or me. You know when someone really likes you and you really like them back. Jenn and I didn't have that, but we were polite. Collegial. And from what Larry said, it didn't sound as if she was being territorial about her husband. She was guarding ...

"Linus," Larry said. "I'm gonna have some words with that guy. If he'd been available right now, I wouldn't be here with you."

I huffed. "Gee, thanks, Lar."

Larry caught up to his blunder. "Sorry. I didn't mean it that way."

"Where is ol' Mr. Travers this evening?" I asked, although the instant I did, a wave of dread crested over me.

"He's on a date," Larry said.

Honesty time: That shook me. Pissed myself off, too, because what business was it of mine what Linus did with his time? None whatsoever. And still ...

"A date," I said. "Good for him." *Maybe.*

"That guy's been spending too much time at our place," Larry said. "He was kind of a project for Jenn, you know? Got his heart broken pretty bad in his divorce, and so we took him in, propped him up. I think it's divided us in a kind of insidious way."

That's when my mind reeled anew. *That's it, of course. Linus.* Why wouldn't Jenn's feelings have crossed the line? Linus was good. Linus was considerate. Linus knew things and had a gentle way about him, a way that made you feel as though he was fully present with you, regardless of how trivial the moment was. I didn't know him from Adam at the New Year's Eve party, but I had a sense about him, even as I approached as the clock struck midnight. I knew I could kiss him. That he'd let me.

Holy shit.

"I'll kick his ass if I have to," Larry said now. "I don't care."

I hurtled back into the moment. "No, I don't think you will."

Larry stood up, as if jolted. "I gotta go."

"Linus," I started. *Dammit!* "Larry," I corrected, "hang on."

"What?" he asked.

"Don't do anything rash with anyone. Think it through. Trust me on that one."

It was as if he hadn't heard a word I'd just said. "What's up with Rex?"

"Nothing. It's over."

"You sure?"

"Beyond sure."

"OK," Larry said. "I'll talk to you soon."

And with that, he was gone.

I stood up and looked around, as if I'd been dropped onto some strange street corner.

I went outside, got in the car, and drove home. No music. No talking to myself. No checking the phone. Just me and the thump of my own heart in my chest.

As I turned right on First Avenue North downtown, I saw Linus's truck at a parking meter, and I wondered where he'd gone tonight and whom he was with and why I cared.

Linus

Mr. Teacher Man

I WENT OUT WITH SARI AGAIN A FEW NIGHTS LATER. This time we went more upscale with dinner at Walkers. Dressed for the occasion. She in a black "date dress," as she called it. Apparently women have what they call a "little black dress" for all occasions. She looked downright sexy in it. Sari was curvy. I like curves. I wore slacks and a dress shirt left over from my teaching days. No tie.

"Well," she said when she saw me, drawing it out teasingly. We'd decided to meet at the venue again. "Don't you clean up good, Mr. Teacher Man."

"You mean Mr. Contractor Man."

She crinkled her nose and squinted. "You really don't look like a contractor."

"What do contractors look like?"

"I don't know. Rugged."

"I'm not rugged?"

"You're cute," she said just before we were seated and she ordered a glass of wine.

"Just cute?" I was trying to be flirty to hide my disappointment but fooling no one. She played along, at least.

"Oh yeah. Totally cute. Like, if you were my teacher, I would have had a crush on you. How many of your students had a crush on you?"

"I never counted," I said. This was dangerous ground, even in retrospect. A few possibly did, and with those I had to go into lockdown-and-don't-even-think-of-saying-anything-that-even-remotely-encourages-them mode. Those episodes were scary then and scary now, and frankly, I'd have preferred we just talked about something else. Like being a contractor.

She laughed as she sensed my unease. "Linus, Linus, Linus." Her twinkling eyes turned mischievous. "What are we going to do with you?"

"I'm open to suggestions," I said.

You know what? I'll just cut to the chase and tell you what we did. After a dinner laced with euphemisms and conversation about sports, and a Nutella ice cream that I'm sure was an aphrodisiac in disguise, we went back to her place (more specifically, I followed her car to her place) and we had sex. Mighty nice sex.

Yes. I defied my friends-first rule. But did I mention that ice cream? And the way she licked her spoon, delightfully *mmmmmmm*-ing with every taste? Plus that little black dress. And her hair. And her smile. And her cleavage. And the way she swirled her tongue around mine when she kissed me on the sidewalk the moment we exited the restaurant. She tasted like wine and ice cream, smelled like vanilla, felt like velvet. She made that *mmmmmmm* sound yet again.

She aroused more than my senses.

It's good to be back in the game.

MEANWHILE, Jennifer hadn't answered a single text since that night we spoke on the phone. Worried something had happened to her, I went to the Morelli house after seeing Sari off to work (her kid had stayed at his dad's house, as if Sari had planned for me to spend the night). I knocked on the door twice and popped it open, calling in as I usually do.

Charlie answered. "In here."

I followed the kiddo's voice into the TV room, where his eyes were fixed on the screen and an intergalactic battle he was waging, his fingers furiously maneuvering the game console.

"Hey buddy," I said. "Where are the parental units?"

"Upstairs, I think," he said, not even blinking in my direction.

"Oh," I said.

"They've been fighting," he said as a space cruiser exploded.

My breakfast turned over inside me.

"About what?" I asked.

Was I asking out of nosiness, or to be an ear for Charlie? He didn't seem fazed, but maybe that was a defense mechanism. I remembered dying a little inside every time my parents fought— even if it wasn't frequent—and feeling the utter helplessness and loneliness of it. Part of that, I'm sure, was being an only child and not having a sibling to help ease the tension of a house on edge. It was the saving grace of Amanda's and my failed marriage—no scarred children.

"About you," Charlie said.

You'd think the kid just hit me with one of his pixelated missiles.

Before I could parse a sentence (or a thought, for that matter), I whipped around at the sound of Larry's booming voice.

"Don't you ever think to call before barging into someone's home?"

Even Charlie was startled, resulting in a direct attack on one of his fleet.

"I ..." Still no words.

Jennifer barreled down the stairs and halted behind him. "Don't you yell at him. He's doing what he always does."

"Exactly," Larry said.

"I ... was worried," I finally stammered. I looked at Jenn. "You didn't answer any of my messages."

She refused to make eye contact with me.

"Why didn't you call *me* and ask how she was?" Larry said.

That was a good question. Why didn't I call him? Especially after he'd called me. I dropped the ball on that, big time.

Of course, that was also the answer. He'd sounded weird when I bailed on his invite to get a beer with him. Agitated and even angry. Frankly, I didn't want to get into it with him.

Or maybe that wasn't it at all.

Maybe I didn't call him because I already knew what he would say.

The tension was thick and rough.

"I'm sorry," I said. "I should have called." I should have called *Larry*. I should have called before I came over. Or maybe I just should have stayed at Sari's. Or gone straight home last night after dinner.

"You should go," said Jenn, her focus on the floor. It was as if she knew where I'd been and what I'd done last night and this morning. "It's not a good time."

I turned around and left without saying another word, except to Charlie. "See ya, kiddo."

Why on earth had they been fighting about me?

On the drive home, I pieced together several truths, some immediate and some that I realized, much to my chagrin, had been brewing for a while:

Jennifer and Larry were in serious trouble.
I was somehow caught in the middle of it.
I was now in a relationship and had no one to tell.
It was snowing again.

When I entered my house, I lost my breakfast. After washing out my mouth and splashing water on my face, I looked in the mirror. For the first time, I saw my age. Wrinkles on my forehead and gray hairs at the temples and bags under my eyes.

How had it all gone to hell so quickly, and when I wasn't looking?

And how was I going to work today when the concentration I'd need had just been scattered to the blustery winds outside?

I looked down at my phone, buzzing across the kitchen countertop.

Jo-Jo Middlebury.

Jo-Jo

God bless the great indoors

I CALLED LINUS FIRST THING WHEN I WOKE UP BECAUSE ... well, because I'd just awakened. Nine-thirty-seven a.m., if you can believe that. I hadn't slept so late since the night after my last final at college, and that was, what, seventeen years ago? A long damn time. I didn't like it. I didn't like sleeping so late, or calling Linus as if he somehow controlled my fate. I didn't like much of anything happening right now.

Because here's the thing: I hadn't been sleeping well, not since Larry and I talked and Linus had taken up residence in my head, where I didn't want him. Or anyone else. So I slept in because I didn't sleep—really and truly sleep—until well into morning.

I can't have this.

Cholly lifted her head, brushed the rug with her tail, then set her chin back on her front paws while Linus's phone rang. As if she were waiting for an answer, too.

"Hi, Jo-Jo," Linus said, when he answered at last. "Miss Middlebury," he corrected. I was getting increasingly irked with the "Miss Middlebury" pretense, even though I was the one who had insisted on it.

"Are you OK?" I asked. "You sound sick." He really did. His words were thick and slurry, like his tongue wasn't working properly, and he was breathing heavily.

"I'm fine."

"You sure?"

"Yeah. What's up?"

I steeled myself. I had some things I needed to say to Linus, and some things I wanted to say, but I wasn't sure if what I wanted to say should be said. That made sense, right?

No. No, it didn't.

Beyond all that, I just wanted to feel like myself again. Tough Jo-Jo, owner of Mighty Jo's Gym. Never in need, punch your problems till they bleed. That's who I wanted to be. And I didn't feel like that woman at all. It was a cumulative thing—my gym, Rex, Larry's problems spilling over into mine. And Linus. I had Linus in my thoughts, and I needed him out.

I bailed right out of the necessary things and the desired things and started with the lamest thing I could possibly say. "How are things going?"

"Fine. Great."

"Where are you?" I asked. I sat up in bed, suddenly aware of something that didn't compute.

"At the gym. Where else?"

"Bullshit."

"Bullshit?"

"I don't hear the whoosh of traffic from the street," I said. "I don't hear the echo of your voice in that big empty space. So where are you?"

I was pissed. Nothing I hate more than a liar. But was I pissed simply because Linus hadn't been truthful, or was I pissed because of where he might be? I decline to answer on the grounds that it might make me feel even more out of sorts.

"I'm at home," he said. "But I'm heading in now. Sorry, I had some things come up, and I meant to be there by now."

"So you're late," I pressed. "Should I be concerned?"

"About what?"

"About my gym," I said. "You promised me you'd get this thing done."

"Yes, I did," he said, about as sharply as I'd ever heard him say anything. "And I'm going to deliver. Don't you worry about it."

"Well, I am worried."

"Well, suit yourself. We've got the locker rooms tiled and most of the fixtures in. Which you'd know if you'd been around the last couple of days."

I bolted out of bed. Cholly gathered herself and followed me out of the bedroom.

"Well," I said, "maybe I'd have been there if somebody hadn't kicked me out of my own gym."

"The hell I did," he said.

"The hell you didn't, Linus."

I waited for another volley from him. My synapses fired. I *wanted* another volley from him. I wanted him to say something else, and I would rush in on his words and crush them. Crush him. That's what I wanted.

I waited some more. Nothing but his breathing and mine.

And, finally, the real voice of Linus Travers—the voice I knew—came across the line.

"Miss Middlebury, I'm sorry," he said, and the fight went right out of me, as if someone had pulled a plug and all my aggressiveness and gumption had drained out onto the floor.

"You can call me Jo-Jo, you know."

"I never meant for you to stay away for good," he went on, seemingly deaf or indifferent to my offer, "but I can see how it must have seemed like that to you. I'm truly sorry. That was not my intent, but however it felt to you counts for more than what I intended. It's your gym. Come by any time. We've got good stuff to show you."

What just happened?

"OK," I said. "Tomorrow. I don't feel so good today."

"I hope it's nothing serious."

"It's not."

"OK, Miss Middlebury."

"Come on, Linus. Just call me Jo-Jo. Take care of yourself. I'll see you soon."

I hung up.

Seriously, what the hell just happened?

FOR THE NEXT HOUR AND A HALF, I worked out my frustration on the elliptical machine, the one now in my living room but destined for my office at the gym. "Workout" was a fitting word for exercise. I'd put untold miles on that thing, sweating out my troubles with men—and Rex—and anxiety, the scary decision to leave my office management job, increase my hours as a personal trainer, and launch my gym, and everything else that seemed to come at me. When it was just me and the elliptical, everything in the world seemed sensible and right. We'd been through a lot together, and Cholly lounged on the floor in front of me, where I could see her and watch her ears perk as I said, "One mile, girl," and "Two miles, girl," and so on.

That simple piece of machinery—I'd had it overhauled twice in four years, so considerable was the wear I put on it—had been the one extravagance I'd allowed myself in all those years of saving every extra dollar and dime for Mighty Jo's Gym. I'd bypassed vacations I'd wanted to take, nights out with friends who gradually stopped inviting me, good cheese, you name it, just to save money and prepare myself for something I was now, at long last, tantalizingly close to realizing. Even when Rex said he wanted to get married—*HA!*—I made him promise we'd get plain rings. Nothing fancy. "I'd just as soon put the money toward the gym," I'd said, and he'd agreed. Of course he had. He never intended to get married, so what's a cheap ring to him?

So what was this morning's frustration? Take your pick. My friend Larry was hurting, and it was possibly my fault. I was mad at my contractor because he went on a date. I was mad at me for being mad at my contractor because he went on a date. I was mad at Rex for coming back so soon after dumping me, and at me (again) for not telling him to keep on walking. I was mad because I'd gotten engaged to the slug in the first place.

I was so sick of the black cloud of drama that followed me everywhere I went.

Then again, maybe I was giving the cloud too much credit. After all, what was *my* role in all this? Didn't I hold Rex—and everyone else—at arm's length? Wasn't I the one to set the terms with Linus? Had I really not been considerate of Jenn's feelings for the duration of her relationship with Larry, and instead placed an unfair expectation on her to accept *my* relationship with Larry? Was drama really some sort of roulette wheel where the marble just so happened to fall on my number every time, or had I rigged that game from the start? Drama happened because I expected it. Because I recognized it.

I suddenly yearned to know the other side. Like desperately yearned. Hungered and thirsted for it.

I'D JUST COME BACK INTO THE LIVING ROOM AFTER MY SHOWER AND A FRESH change of clothes when I heard two quick knuckle raps against the door. I looked up to see Rex with his face pressed against the glass, looking in.

Oh, come on. Really?

"Jo-Jo," he said, his voice muffled by the door between us. "Open up."

I made for the door. "Say please," I said.

"C'mon, Jo-Jo, it's a friggin' tundra out here."

"And ...?"

He huffed and blew out steam. "May I please come in?"

I opened the door, but only enough so we could speak.

"Can I come in?" he asked.

"Nope."

"Seriously?" he said. I looked past him to the street. January in Billings, Montana. White sky. White ground. White swirls on the wind. I loved it.

"Should have thought of that before you dropped by unannounced," I said.

Rex made his irritating little puppy-dog face. Two months ago, I would have bought it. Not today. Not anymore.

"You're mad," he said.

"I'm indifferent."

"What is that supposed to mean?"

"Rex, go away."

He gathered himself and tried again. "I bought you flowers. Did you get them?"

"I did."

He smiled expectantly. "And?"

"You think flowers make it all better?"

His expression soured. "OK, so what does make it all better?"

"Nothing. Your leaving was the solution. Believe me, you did the right thing, Rex. It was never going to be what we pretended it was."

Rex wasn't allowing it. "Geezus, Jo-Jo. I'm trying here."

I just looked at him. No. That's not it. I looked *through* him.

"Trying to do what?" I asked.

He looked utterly confused by the question.

"To … to get you back."

"Rex, I'm trying to tell you. You never had me in the first place. You said didn't want to be married to me. Whatever led you to that conclusion was the right one, because neither one of us was all in. We were settling. You didn't make a mistake, you did a courageous thing. I only wish we'd both been brave enough before we threw all that money away on a venue and photographer and invitations. I wish we hadn't taken so many people down with us."

We looked in each other's eyes. and it was as if the truth had finally appeared to us in full Technicolor. Only it wasn't some kind of euphoric enlightenment. It was a profound sadness as thick as molasses. I suddenly, inexplicably, wanted to dive headfirst into it.

Cholly stood and came to the door, curious, which snapped Rex and me out of our gaze and out of the moment. And it was as if the moment had never happened, and he was right back to being consciously asleep. "Hi, girl," he said as his eyes lit up upon sight of her. He wiggled his fingers low through the opening. She licked them. "Can I at least see Cholly?"

"Rex," I pleaded. "Please."

And just like that, he turned on me yet again. "You're a real bitch, you know that?"

I was done.

It should have been over and done the first time he'd called me that. We'd gone out as a foursome—Rex and me and Caroline the cop and one of her one-off dates—and a night of drinking had made him rude and rowdy to everyone at the bar. "You can be such a bitch about stuff," he'd said when I'd called him out on his behavior on the ride home. I was hurt, but I'd let him off the hook because he was drunk and he'd be ashamed of his behavior in the morning, which he was. Thing is, I made excuses for when he called me a bitch when he wasn't drunk.

Rationalization is a terrible trick of the mind.

I was going to marry a man who called me a bitch. That sadness barreled into me again. How could I have purported to love Rex so much while loving myself so little?

I straightened my posture and spoke with commanding power. Not anger, not sass, not defensiveness, but honest-to-God power. "No, I'm not. And I will never allow you to call me that again. A person who truly loves me and wants to be with me would never dare call me that."

A thought followed: *Linus would never call me that.*

I was about to slam the door on him. "OK, OK," he said, "I'm sorry." He'd said that every other time he'd called me a bitch. Impatiently. Dismissively. Never genuinely.

"Rex," I said, practically begging. "Are you even listening to yourself?"

He paused, bewildered, and then he blinked rapidly a few times and focused, as if he woke up and didn't know what he was doing in my doorway.

It's over.

I nudged Cholly back, and closed the door without saying another word. Drew the shade across the glass. Turned and walked away.

Relieved.

I returned to the bedroom, sat on the bed, and stroked Cholly's head, while I took deep breaths and allowed tears to roll down my cheeks. Ten minutes later, I padded back to the front door and opened it. A set of deep footprints led away, out to the street. I stood in the cold and watched hypnotically as the snow fell, filling them in, until finally it was as if Rex had never been here at all.

Mr. Blue Sky

Like the pilgrims, we're making progress

WHERE HAVE I BEEN? I'll tell you where I've been: working overtime, trying to help you avert your numbskull moves (every calamitous event starts with "Hey, watch this ..."), and filling out paperwork in triplicate after you decided to lick an icy light pole because you're drunk.

No, no, not *you*. But somebody. All the time. Forever.

But let's not dwell on my day. We have other things to discuss.

Let's consider Mr. Travers and Miss Middlebury, who suddenly wants to drop the formality. Circumstances have changed, haven't they? I dare say we've reached the "it's complicated" stage, as if all of life can be boiled down into neat little social media status selections.

How encouraging or discouraging all of this is depends greatly on your perspective and allegiances. To put it in your vernacular, if you're Team Linus, there's reason for optimism and concern. He's "back in the game," in his words, and that's what he wanted for this young year. He also still has significant boundary problems, which is why he defied his own rule by sleeping with Sari on the second date. Moreover, Jennifer is projecting a lot of her own issues onto him, and because he feels indebted to her for past support, he's inclined to take ownership of them. And Larry might cave his face in, for obvious reasons.

If you're Team Jo-Jo, you might be celebrating her final dismissal of Rex. And now, she's discovering that she has actual feelings lurking under all that Lycra and rage. Specifically, she has feelings for Linus, and right now they're surprising and confusing her. This is what happens when you set things in motion. All of them, on that fateful New Year's Eve, did so in their own way and their own intentions. When the universe responds, you need to be prepared for all the stuff that gets stirred up in the process. And that stuff needs to get stirred up. Whether they consciously knew it or not, some part of them wanted it stirred up. Needed it, in fact.

All endings—even those that are for the best, those that aren't endings but rather completions—are losses. And they need to be grieved.

Jo-Jo still hasn't grieved. And she needs to, pronto. She's not going to really move forward until she does.

I'll go one step further and say this: She's not going to get anywhere, with herself or anybody else, until she opens herself to trust. Did you catch her disarmament when Linus apologized to her? He took responsibility for what he said and did, and he left it to Jo-Jo to take responsibility for her own words and feelings. That's smart and healthy. She's never seen that before, not from a man, anyway, and she doesn't yet know what to do with it. But something sunk in, because look at how she responded to Rex's attempt at an apology. She saw it for what it was, which wasn't an apology at all—

at least not in the remorseful way—but rather an attempt to control. Rex wanted to go back to the familiar, because *he* didn't like what he had set in motion when he called things off with Jo-Jo. And she's finally realizing that she's not the victim of her circumstances as much as she's an enabler of it. Good for her for not getting sucked back into that false comfort.

You may look at all this—Linus and Jo-Jo and Jennifer and Larry and Rex and Amanda and Sari (there's a feisty one!)—and see it all as hopelessly fraught.

Mr. Blue Sky sees something else.

This is the process. This is life and how you live it.

This, to be precise, is the gift.

Now, give Mr. Blue Sky a gift and mosey along. One of my charges had a close call with a deer while driving home, despite my very clear whispering in his ear to remember TO WATCH FOR DEER AT NIGHT IN WINTER.

The guy is fine. So is the deer. His truck is not, having swerved and fishtailed into a fence.

Sadly, it doesn't always end so well. Happens every winter.

Sometimes humanity is a perpetual case of a toddler's defiance. "Don't touch that, Timmy. You'll burn yourself." Timmy touches it anyway.

It's how you learn mindfulness. And how not to be a dumbass.

But now I have to file a report, and *Barney Miller* is about to come on. It's one thing after another around here.

Linus

Waiting for spring ...

I THINK I MADE A MISTAKE. With Sari, that is.

Don't get me wrong—Sari is wonderful. She's funny and energetic and a good mom and good in bed. But that's the problem—not that she's good in bed (how could that ever be a problem?) but that I went to bed with her too soon, especially after saying I didn't want to have that kind of relationship. I really did want to take things slowly. But it's been a month and now we're, like, in a relationship, and I feel like I'm walking on pins and needles all the time. Like I'm playing a role of "boyfriend" rather than just being me. What's more, I don't know how to get out of it. Because I don't want to get out of it, really. I just can't go back and start over the way I'd wanted to—cultivating that friendship and then gradually building to intimacy. There's no way I can say, "Can we just be friends, Sari?" without it sounding like I'm about to dump her. And, confession time, I *like* the sex.

More than that, I like how the sex happens, how Sari initiates it at least as often as I do, how she reaches for me and is playful—"You only need one tool for this job" was a recent, hilarious declaration as she removed my work belt—and is all about the fun. I've never had that before.

But damn. I made a mistake.

That's not the only mistake I made. Neither Jennifer nor Larry was speaking to me. Or each other. I'd made the mistake of going back to their house—again unannounced—hoping I could talk things over with them, get things out in the open, find out exactly what role I had played in their problems. It was *Dungeons and Dragons* night at Charlie's friend Stewie's house, and I knew Charlie would be spending the night there.

Larry had started. "Tell him, Jenn. Tell him how you wish he'd slept with you rather than Sally."

Holy shit.

"Sari," I said sheepishly.

"Whatever," Larry said.

Jennifer sat on the couch and stared at her lap.

I fixed my gaze on her, trying to get her to look up. The living room suddenly felt suffocatingly small. "Jenn, have you developed feelings for me?"

"Damn right," Larry said.

I shot him an angry look. "I want *her* to say it."

Jenn shot back. "I'm not saying anything. Will both of you stop ganging up on me?"

I was startled. "You could have talked to me about this," I said to her. "I'm on your side."

"Of course you are," Larry said.

"Oh, will you shut up?" Jenn yelled at him. "You're not exactly pure in all this. Why aren't you telling Linus the *real* reason you're mad at him?"

Why else could he possibly be mad at me?

Larry pressed his lips together and formed fists, his knuckles turning white.

"No? Nothing to say now?" Jenn said. "OK, well, since you told Linus all about my feelings, I'll tell him all about yours. For Jo-Jo. The woman you *really* wanted to marry. How you hate Linus for taking a liking to her. How you hate that she kissed *him* on New Year's Eve. How you hate that *he's* the one taking care of her right now and not you."

It was a rhetorical question, dammit.

"That's not true," Larry said, the sharpness of his tone betraying his words.

One thing wasn't true. I wasn't taking care of her. In fact, the following day I was going to have to break my promise to her about having the gym ready by Presidents' Day.

I gaped at both of them. One minute we were a trio—Lar and Jenn and Linus—and the next minute we were ... a triangle. I still couldn't wrap my head over how and why it had imploded without any warning sign.

Then again, had I shown them any warning signs before Amanda and I split? No. They had been shocked when she and I broke the news to them. Because most of the energy you're expending isn't trying to hide the problems from your friends. It's trying to hide them from yourself.

It hit me: Jennifer and Larry's marriage had been on fire long before New Year's Eve. Maybe that was the reason for the jar full of resolutions. Maybe they were setting their own timetable, giving themselves a year to contain the inferno, get it under control, and then fix it. But my experience was that you're already way past the expiration date before you even set one.

It wasn't about me.

Or maybe it was.

AND THEN THERE WAS JO-JO. Not that I hadn't tried to keep my promise. I really, really had—I had worked twelve-hour days, weekends, but I just couldn't get it done. Who knew it was going to snow *every single day for seventeen days straight*? And who knew the City Council had voted the year before to slash road-plowing services from the budget during fiscal planning? Roads got jammed up. The airport got jammed up. Suppliers got jammed up. I spent a good chunk of time every day just shoveling out the entrances and parking lot.

After a sleepless night following the Larry and Jennifer Shit-Show (we had all agreed to cease communicating for some time), Jo-Jo knew what I was going to tell her. I'd brought her a chocolate chip muffin and a cup of raspberry tea to soften the blow.

"So you're going to tell me that I wasted my advertising dollars on yet another grand opening that isn't going to happen," she said before I even handed her the consolation goodies.

Maybe you shouldn't have been so confident, I'd wanted to say. But she had a right to be disappointed. Even upset.

"Jo-Jo, I am truly sorry," I started, my voice quavering. It was the same feeling as when I had to tell a student that despite his best efforts and mine, he wouldn't pass the class or graduate with his friends. Like ripping their heart out of their chest, and then ripping out my own so it would have company. "I really thought I could get it done. But the damn snow ..."

"Yeah, yeah, yeah," she interjected. "Mother Nature hates my ass."

"I'm sure she has no opinion either way."

She eyed me coldly. I'd meant it as a joke.

I looked around the place. Structurally, it was complete, and it was gorgeous. Matted flooring in the equipment rooms, hardwoods in in the exercise rooms, tiles in the locker rooms, and industrial carpet in the lobby. Wall-to-wall windows on one side, mirrors on the other. Deluxe sound system. Soundproof rooms for individual classes. Spa-like locker rooms consisting of saunas and mosaic-tiled showers and bright red lockers that you could unlock by scanning your lanyard. Murals of seascapes, canyons, forests, mountaintops ... anywhere in nature you wanted to be. What was missing consisted of equipment, computers, things that were snowed in at some warehouse. Things that were completely beyond my control, and hers.

Didn't stop her from blaming me, though.

"You shouldn't have promised me," she said. "That was your mistake. And my mistake was trusting you."

"First of all, I *didn't* promise you," I started. "Remember? You were skeptical of promises. So instead I offered to do the best I could. And second, some things are simply out of the realm of a promise. It didn't make my intention to keep that promise any less sincere. Everything I could control got done on time."

"You did promise," she insisted. "You *promised*." As I started to object, she held up a hand. "You know what? Forget it. Just forget it. It's my fault. Maybe one of these days I'll finally learn." She turned on her heel to walk away, but I wasn't having it.

"Finally learn what?"

"That no one in this world is reliable."

Then she turned her back on me. And I blew a gasket.

I jogged ahead and blocked her path. "Hold on," I said.

"Back off, Linus."

"No, Jo-Jo, I won't. I spent the last five weeks busting my ass—I got up two hours earlier and left two hours later. I worked Saturdays. I paid my subcontractors overtime and didn't charge you for it." The volume of my voice escalated with the level of my anger. "My own house is a series of unfinished walls and wiring, and my calendar is frozen because I made Mighty Jo's Gym my one and only priority. I was even planning to absorb the costs you invested in advertising.

And you have the nerve—the *gall*—to call me *unreliable*. How dare you!"

She stared at me, a storm raging in her eyes, yet she didn't say a word. So I finished.

"The problem, Miss Middlebury, is not that the world is unreliable, because it isn't. The problem is that you don't rely on it for anything. And maybe I did act as if I'd promised you that the gym would be ready when I said it would, and I shouldn't have. Only because I wanted it as much as you did."

I wanted other things, too. I wanted everything to go back to normal with my two best friends. I wanted my girlfriend to not be my girlfriend until I was ready for her to be my girlfriend. I'd never wanted my marriage to end, either.

But was any of that what I *really* wanted? I mean, where was *I* in all of this? Was I an active participant in my own life, or had I been leaning against a wall watching it from day one?

Suddenly, I didn't want any of it.

I left Jo-Jo, agog, and cautiously drove on slick, snowpacked roads to my house, where I proceeded to take a sledgehammer to the new walls I'd put up and tear them down again.

Mr. Blue Sky

Whoa

ARE YOU PAYING ATTENTION? This is huge, folks.

Spoiler alert: A light just went on in Jo-Jo. Linus gave her some hard truths about how she approaches the world with a raised fist rather than open arms. And I don't mind telling you I wrapped my presence around her in that moment. She might have collapsed otherwise, and she needed to feel that assurance, that grace.

As for Linus, the walls are crashing down. Literally.

Good.

As the cool kids say, shit's getting real, folks.

Jo-Jo

Trust is a four-letter word

IT'S HARD TO DESCRIBE WHAT I FELT WHEN LINUS TOLD ME THAT I DON'T LET anyone in. Wait, no, that's not what he said; that's what I *got* from what he said, which isn't the same thing.

He said he didn't promise me, because I had told him not to. Said I don't rely on the world for anything, and that cut me as deeply as anything that's ever been said to me. Not because it was mean or unfair.

Because it was true. Because I knew it was true.

Because, and God knows how strange this is for me to say, it was a loving thing to say.

My knees all but buckled at his words, and then, as if someone slipped his arms underneath mine and propped me up, I was present and safe, and I was thankful.

Thankful.

And then Linus went off and running to his truck and was gone.

I FOUND HIM AT HIS HOUSE, across the street from my old house. There I was, back in that part of town I swore I'd never visit again, for the second time in just a few weeks. And there he was, in his living room, tearing out the walls.

I didn't knock. I opened the door and stepped in, and he went on with the sledgehammer, ferociously oblivious.

"You'll get a more powerful swing if you balance your weight better," I said.

He looked up, startled and wild-eyed through his safety goggles. "Jo-Jo."

"Mr. Travers."

I stepped toward him, my hand out. "May I show you?"

He handed me the hammer wordlessly, then stepped back. I held it in both hands, assessing its weight. I spread my legs as if in a fighting stance. I did what I longed to advise my gym clients to do, if the day ever came when I'd actually have some: I generated my power from the bottom of my feet, through my legs and core, and out to my hands, and I sent the hammer crashing into the wall in a cloud of shattered drywall and dust.

"Like that," I said. I swung again. "Like that." Again. "Like that."

Linus reached for my shoulder, and I stopped.

"Let me try," he said.

I relinquished the hammer, though I so wanted to keep going.

He mimicked my stance. Good footwork. Knees bent. I took note of how trim he was; a little soft in places, for sure, but well-put-together. I'd never noticed before. But right there ... Damn. Linus was downright attractive.

He swung, and a huge section of wall cratered. "Like that?" he asked, looking to me.

"Like that."

He swung again. We passed the hammer like a baton every three or four swings, and that wall came down in no time.

LINUS DUG A COUPLE OF PABST BLUE RIBBONS OUT OF THE REFRIGERATOR, and we clinked bottles while we sat on his front porch, watching the incessant snow fall lazily, translucent in the streetlights. Toby the cat stayed on the other side of the door, occasionally standing on his back legs and pressing his front paws against the glass of the storm door, watching us. Odd, he had kind of the same facial expressions as Linus.

"I feel like we should be having hot buttered rum or something," Linus said. "Awfully cold out for this."

I tugged at the loose corner of the bottle's label. "I like it. Peaceful. And, hey, I'm always up for redneck champagne."

Linus laughed. "That's a new one for me."

I clinked his bottle again. "Glad I could expand your horizons."

He fell in beside me a contented sigh. "I'm sorry for being so harsh earlier," he said.

"Don't be. You weren't."

Linus lay back, resting his back against the upper step, stretching his legs out so his booted feet dangled over the bottom one. I scanned up the street and down. Quiet, nobody out. Winter evenings past flooded into my memories, most of them wrapped in silence like this one. A lot of people in Billings have this concept of the South Side as a festering den of drug use and crime. I worked with a guy once who said he wouldn't go to that side of town at night, as if there were monsters here rather than blue-collar have-nots. Total flake, that guy. The horrors I knew here weren't on the streets; they were behind the walls of my own home. And that would have been true no matter where we lived, because of the way we lived. That's what I had run from. The pathology, not the geography.

I pointed across the park at the row of houses. "I grew up there," I said.

Linus sat up, intent. "Which one? The green one?"

"No, the white one next to it."

"That was your house?" He sounded almost awed.

"That was my house."

"Wow. I had no idea."

"Of course you didn't. How could you?"

I looked at him and braved a smile. He looked back at me in a way that told me I didn't have to say anything else, unless I really wanted to. As if he'd heard me and intuited the rest, which is exactly what I needed from him.

"Why did you decide to open a gym?" he asked, and I didn't see that one coming.

"How long do you have?"

"As long as it takes."

It wasn't much of a story, to be honest, but I relished the chance to tell it. "I first had the idea in college," I said. "I took an exercise class—"

"At MSU Billings?"

"Yeah," I said. "Anyway, I was good at it. And I lost a lot of weight. A lot of weight. Everything felt right when I exercised, and everything felt off when I didn't. You know? I started getting into the efficiency of it, how I could maximize a half-hour, really get a good burn going, how I could keep my balance on what I ate and how I exercised. And the control was entirely with me."

"Simple math," he said. "Fuel in, energy out."

"Yeah." *Yeah, exactly.* "Anyway, I wanted to be able to transfer that knowledge, that drive, to somebody who needs it the way I needed it."

Linus seemed to take this all in and roll it around in his head. I'd come to appreciate that about him, that all the responses weren't automatic or rote. He thought before he spoke. Most of the time.

"You need to have this gym," he said. "And Billings needs you to have this gym."

Had anything ever touched me more? I didn't think so.

"And you," I deflected. "Why contracting and not teaching?"

Linus set his beer down.

"I'll always be a teacher," he said. "That doesn't go away. But maybe six, seven years into it, I realized something."

"What?"

He picked the beer up again took a swig. "What I wanted to do was teach kids math, and maybe something about growing up if they paid attention to me beyond the coursework," he said. "What I think my administrators wanted me to do, what the community wanted, was something more on the order of social integration. Too much of my time was spent on trying to get these diverse kids—and Jo-Jo, they're really just this amazing collection of perspectives and backgrounds and talents—to coalesce into little automatons. Do you follow me?"

I thought maybe I did. "I don't know."

"Come in the kitchen for a sec."

Linus led me back into the house, to the still-unfinished kitchen where I'd once eaten Mrs. Crater's pancakes. He pointed to a long piece of fabricated wood leaning against the wall. "See that backsplash?" he asked. "When I get to it, I'm going to have to make that straight piece of wood mold to that wall over there." He pointed to the area behind the sink. "That wall is crooked."

"Crooked?"

"Yes, all walls are crooked. The lumber dries and warps, and they get crooked. That's life. So I'm going to set that backsplash against the wall, and I'm going to put adhesive to it, and it's not going to form-fit that crooked wall. So I'll take some shims and I'll apply pressure wherever I have to—to the side, from above, wherever—

and I'll force that piece of wood to bend to that crooked wall. And my point is that I just realized, after a few years of teaching, that I'd rather bend straight things to an askew world than take some wonderfully askew kid and try to make him bend to a world that won't celebrate his uniqueness."

Holy ...

"And I also just realized that one beer makes me come up with completely absurd analogies," Linus added.

It took me another minute to reel myself in. Linus smiled awkwardly at me, and I smiled awkwardly right back.

I finally knew what all those books and movies were talking about when they said time stood still in that instant you make eye contact, and you're just completely locked in to the present moment, where there's no one and nothing but the two of you. No baggage. No pain. No fear. And you feel like you're seeing the other person. Like, really *seeing* them. And they see you, and know you, and for once in your life you're OK with it.

"The gym will be done when it's done," I said at last. "I have the right man for the job."

I suddenly felt light enough to float into the sky. Like some emotional barbell fell off me and clattered away. I actually wiggled my toes to make sure they were still on the ground.

Linus leaned toward me—close enough for me to feel his breath—and my heart pounded and my veins coursed with current and little pins and needles danced up my spine.

But before he could get any closer, I felt myself crashing back into my body. My muscles twitched, enough that Linus noticed. He pulled away and furrowed his brows in a worried frown.

"Are you OK?" he asked.

Good question. *Was I? What the hell just happened?*

I kicked things back to the mundane. "Any chance I could use that beautiful bathroom of yours?"

"Sure thing," he said, visibly disappointed. "You know the way, right?"

"I'll be back in a second."

I DIDN'T HAVE TO GO. I had to think.

Linus was about to kiss me.

I wanted him to.

I wanted to kiss him back. And again and again.

He's a good man, Linus Travers.

But despite what I'd felt in that moment, he doesn't know me yet—not really—and I don't know him the way I need to before there's anything more. *If* there's anything more.

Or so I thought.

I flushed the toilet.

I washed my hands.

I looked at myself in the mirror.

He wanted to kiss me.

I want him to kiss me. I want him to want me.

I turned off the light, and I stepped out of the bathroom. Toby skitted past me and into Linus's bedroom. Before I reached the living room, I heard voices, plural. Linus's, and a woman's.

I rounded the corner and headed toward the open door. Linus stood on his porch wearing an expression that said "hell of an interesting situation we've got here," and a woman about our age stood, fists on hips, looking at me as if she wanted me dead.

"Jo-Jo, this is Sari," he said. "My ... my girlfriend, I guess."

Linus

Right away you're starting off bad

I KNEW I WAS GOING TO CATCH HELL THE MOMENT THE WORDS HAD DRIBBLED from my lips, without putting my brain on notice.

"You guess?" Sari said, incredulous. "*You guess?*"

"I should go," Jo-Jo said as she zipped her coat and headed for the door.

"Not just yet," Sari said. "Who are you?"

She extended her hand. "Jo-Jo Middlebury. I'm Linus's client. He's finishing up my gym."

"Is your gym going to be in his living room?" Sari then looked around, finally noticing the rubble of drywall that surrounded us. So did I, come to think of it. What had possessed me?

She frowned. "Seriously, Linus. What is going on in here?"

"Sari—" Fortunately I shut down the impulse to say *It's not what you think*. "Jo-Jo and I ... well, it's been a tough day. I had to break the bad news that her gym wasn't going to be ready on time. We had words. I left. She came to apologize. It was a rather nice thing to do."

Come to think of it, Jo-Jo never actually said the words *I'm sorry*. But I knew that's why she had come. And, frankly, what wasn't said had made all the difference. Even if that moment in the kitchen, right before she used the bathroom, did confuse the hell out of me and put me in hot water with Sari. Maybe Jennifer was right. Drama followed Jo-Jo wherever she went. And who wants to be sucked into that tornado day in and day out?

Only it didn't feel like drama in that moment. That moment when we looked at each other and leaned in. That moment when her wall had come down and she'd invited me in. I was about to kiss her. It felt perfect.

And then, a split-second later, the wall went right back up again.

Had I imagined the moment? Had I misread the signal?

Sari looked at me earnestly. "I'm not the jealous type, Linus. But you haven't answered my messages all day, so when I decided to surprise you with dinner ..."

And it was for the first time that I noticed she was holding a sack of fried chicken from Albertsons. Don't laugh; I love their chicken. They make a pretty good birthday cake, too.

Well, dammit, that was a rather nice thing to do, too.

Jo-Jo started to open her mouth, but I cut her off. "There's no reason for you to be jealous," I said to Sari. "I had my phone off because I was working all day. And I came home in such a huff that I forgot to turn it back on. You're so thoughtful to bring dinner, especially my favorite. Come here."

I opened my arms and she hesitated, contemplating her next move. Time slowed to a near stop, and I panicked in that endless second. I really didn't want to lose Sari from my life. But I didn't want our relationship to be what it was, either. I was more confused than ever.

She went into my arms, and the sack bumped against my lower back. Jo-Jo let herself out. Didn't even say goodbye, which was understandable. In any case, I was relieved she was gone. And sorry.

"I'm really sorry," I said, and I kissed Sari on her forehead before moving to her lips. "I didn't mean to make you worried. Or doubtful."

"Let's eat … somewhere," she said. I looked over my shoulder. The master bedroom and bathroom were still intact, and the kitchen was usable for sitting, but the air was dusty and chaotic. The thought of going driving on the snowy roads didn't appeal, either, but there really was no other choice.

"I have an idea," I said.

We got in my car, and I carefully drove us downtown to the Northern Hotel. The rooms were expensive, but it was the least I could do to remedy the situation. Besides, it would make for a romantic date. Maybe that's what I—*we*—needed. *Romance.* We had skipped that part after sex so soon. Maybe that's what I had been missing all along. Sure, I taught math and was mainly a left-brained guy. I dug football and contact sports. But take me to a movie with a *happily ever after* and I was a puddle. Romance was the outlier. I believed in happily ever after. I believed in destiny and synchronicity and *the one*. Or at least, I had, years ago. I also believed in flowers and candles and little teddy bears and Hallmark cards. Not as clichés, but as surprises. Not for anniversaries, but for Tuesdays.

Oddly, Amanda used to tell me I was romantic in a way that suggested I was wishy-washy, or less macho. If I was ever "macho" for even one minute of my life. (Do people even still use that word?)

I became ashamed. Hid it like an ugly scar. And then I lost it in the divorce, along with so many other things.

It was time to get it back.

Sari approved of this plan.

We entered a mini-suite consisting of a couch and table, master bath with an enormous shower (nice tile work!), and a king-size bed. I went to the window and looked at the landscape of the city. I missed seeing the colorful Christmas lights everywhere, along with menorahs and wreaths and battery-operated candles placed in windows. The treetops were dusted with white, like powdered sugar on cake; it looked so pretty, so peaceful. But it was also deceptive. Behind how many of those doors were couples fighting? How many were full of children who didn't have enough to eat? Of students who were struggling to keep up with the work they were expected to do? Of seniors worried their health insurance wasn't going to cover their medical expenses? I pressed my face against the window, and the glass fogged up.

I couldn't have imagined it. Jo-Jo had wanted to kiss me, too.

But now I didn't want to want it. Or her. I wanted to want Sari, this beautiful, vivacious, funny, drama-free woman. She had so many ways of expressing herself and so few insecurities. Or so it seemed. Maybe I didn't know her as well as I thought I did. Maybe she didn't want me to. Maybe I should be glad this was so uncomplicated. At the moment, it was the most uncomplicated thing in my life. This room. This meal. This view.

We ate without the TV on, and I listened as Sari told me all about her day (I had made certain to ask). Her son, who was staying with his dad that night, aced his social studies test; her boss had blamed her for something her co-worker had screwed up; a pair of shoes she found online for half-price. I was trying so hard to pay attention, to do more than nod, to engage. But my brain was busy replaying my own day—my confrontation with Jo-Jo at the gym, going home and knocking out all the walls in my house ... seriously, why had I done that? Especially after putting so much work into it? It wasn't starting over from scratch, but it was a setback and a mess.

Or maybe it was a chance to do it better the second time around.

And then seeing Jo-Jo right in front of me, as if she'd materialized in response to my erratic thoughts. Taking the sledgehammer from me, showing me the proper stance—she packed a mean pounding with that thing—and the two of us tearing down the wall together. Even with the competing smells of exposed wood and cracked drywall and Pabst and snow, her fragrance flowered every space she was in. That first time we'd been in such close proximity since New Year's Eve, I was practically bowled over by it. And every time I've walked into the gym, I've inhaled and smiled. Like walking into a bakery, where you take in that scent and feel like all is well in your world. But given all the problems that seemed to accompany Jo-Jo and all the chaos that swirled around her, why did it have such a calming effect on me? Why didn't it wreak of crazy?

I suddenly became aware of a hand waving in front of me. "Hello? Earth to Linus ... Come in, Linus ..."

I blinked and looked at Sari. "I'm sorry. I've been kind of frazzled all day."

"I can tell from the looks of your house."

"Yeah, I really don't know what I was thinking. But I wish I had thought, *don't be stupid.*"

Sari leaned into me and inserted her hand between my legs. "So let's not think, then." She kissed me and my body went ablaze and I wanted to do just that—stop thinking and analyzing and poring over all things Jo-Jo Middlebury and just succumb to Sari's sensuous skin and adventurous lips and luscious curves.

I couldn't finish, though.

I apologized profusely—it was the first time my performance had fallen short, so to speak—and Sari ran her fingers up and down my arm, as if to soothe my shame.

"It's really OK, sweet pea," she said. But it wasn't. I knew it. I suspected she knew it.

Moments passed as we lay next to each other in the dark, naked and silent.

"Hey, sweetie?" she piped up softly.

"Yes?" I responded.

"Why did you say you guess?"

It all rushed back at me, and I suddenly wanted to be anywhere but in this bed.

"I just ..." I struggled to find nonconfrontational words. "I guess I'm not sure what this is."

"Us?" she asked.

"Yes."

I braced for tears, anger, something.

"It is what it is," she said. It was so matter-of-fact, so plain, so ... not romantic. The defeat I felt in that moment nearly suffocated me.

"I guess."

We said nothing more, and she fell asleep. I stared out the window, watching the snow, endless and rhythmic, until it lulled me to sleep as well.

Jo-Jo

Time to reset

LINUS HAS A GIRLFRIEND. It's not as though I should have been surprised. At the gym, he's been entirely present when there's been work to do, but he's also been keeping to himself, and to his phone, during lunch breaks. At quitting time, where once he might have lingered to chat about the next phase, he's been loading up his truck and heading out. All reasonable things.

And yet ...

Seeing her—*Sari*, I think she said her name was—proved entirely different than merely knowing she existed. She had a sharp look and a sharper tongue. I don't mean that in a bad way. She was sassy. Normally, I like sassy. But she didn't seem interested in his explanation of what I was doing there. There I go. Judgmental. Had we switched places, I probably wouldn't have been, either.

Yes, I wanted to kiss Linus, and I wanted Linus to kiss me, but what you want and what you ought to get are sometimes poles apart. I knew that when Sari showed up and Linus went out of his way to placate her. I knew it when I excused myself. I don't blame him at all, by the way. How else could he handle that situation? I would've liked to have said goodbye, especially given how we'd set things right between us, but the opportunity wasn't there.

The message here is clear: Linus is my contractor. Nothing more. And I can't allow myself to think about anything more than getting this gym finished and open. Case closed.

Except I can't stop thinking about it. That almost kiss. Linus. Everything.

I CHECKED THE CLOCK—just past 10 a.m.—and I called Caroline the cop on my way home. She has a last name, Grundy, but Caroline the cop honors who she is and what she's about, and the alliteration is a nice touch, too. We met back in freshman comp class in college—she was twenty-four, I was eighteen—and Caroline was on her late-breaking trajectory: a bachelor's degree, the police academy, then the patrol division of the Billings Police Department. I was envious; I was still trying to find my way into a life beyond the home (if you want to call it that) I'd grown up in. In time, I became her de facto coach—her perfect score on the physical portion of her departmental testing was as much mine as it was hers—and she became my no-bullshit friend and confidante. She'd seen me through jobs and relationships and the seeming impossibility of saving enough money to make my gym dream a reality. I'd whipped her back into shape after a pregnancy and a divorce. We had a lot of time in as friends.

"Get back, Jo-Jo," Caroline said upon answering her cell phone, an old joke.

"You coming off shift at midnight?" I asked.

"Same as it ever was."

"I have a bottle of Gewurz."

"How fortunate," she said, chuckling. "I know the way to your house."

WE SAT ON THE FLOOR, a bottle and two glasses and some sliced summer sausage between us, and we moved the pieces of our lives around, in search of answers. We talked about Rex, who I was sure was gone for good now. We talked about Larry, who'd be gone for good if he and Jennifer didn't work things out. We talked about sunken marketing campaigns and the steady erosion of February into March and the narrow margin I now had in my savings account.

On Caroline's side, we talked about her son, Robbie, who'd gone off to Montana State last fall on a football scholarship, and about the joyously dateless life of a middle-aged cop. "I loathe everything about dating," she said. "It would take an extraordinary man to change my mind. Do you know one?"

"Nope," I said.

Wrong! I know one. He won't leave my brain. In fact, he's making a beeline for my heart.

"It's all about the gym," said Caroline, circling back to me, a hint of sarcasm to her words. "That's number one, and everything else is, like, number sixty-three."

"Agreed."

"How's this guy working out for you?" she asked.

I sat up straight. "What?"

"Robiskey kept telling you it was on the verge of getting done, too, and it never got done. Is he shooting straight?"

And then I exhaled. "Oh. Right. No, Linus is the real deal."

She narrowed her eyes. "You sure?"

"You should see the gym," I said. "It's perfect. It's on time and on budget. He did everything he could do. It's not his fault the computer system has been on a loading platform in Kentucky for three days."

"I suppose not."

"It's going to get done. Promise."

Caroline reached for the bottle and poured herself a second glass. "That's some kind of name. Linus." She took it out for a spin. "Wine us and dine us, Linus. It's a Linus rhyme-us."

"You're drunk," I said.

"Not even close."

"He's a good man. I can't wait to show you what he's done."

"He's a good *contractor*," Caroline corrected.

"That's what I meant."

"Right. And I'm the one who's drunk."

I whittled off a hunk of sausage and popped it in my mouth. Caroline peered at me through eye slits. She leaned in.

"You like him, this Linus."

"I do not."

"You do!"

"Finish your wine."

I pushed myself to my feet and wandered to the kitchen table, inundated again with unanswered mail. Overtaken by a sense of urgency, I began to sort the envelopes into three categories— personal, active bills, junk—and prioritize each. Behind me, I heard Caroline stand up and approach.

"Jo-Jo, talk to me."

"I've got mail."

"Jo-Jo," she said again, this time with a sort of belligerent concern. My eyes began welling up. I know how messed up this is, but crying scares me. Not the way clowns scare me, but in the way that it melts down my armor and makes me completely vulnerable. One of my mother's boyfriends had relentlessly taunted me until I finally cried. That's when he knew he'd broken me. That's when he knew he had all the power. And that, incidentally, is when I left home and stayed at my guidance counselor's house for three days.

I had forgotten about that.

I'd also been crying a lot lately. Or so it seemed.

I dropped the mail and covered my face.

"Hey," Caroline took me into her arms; that's when the waterworks exploded.

"I just ... I can't do this anymore," I said.

"Do what?"

"Fail."

Caroline let go, taken aback. "Where have you failed?"

"Everything. My entire life. I just can't seem to figure out how to fix it. First, I thought it was getting an education. Then I thought it was getting a good job. Then I thought it was getting my own business. Then I thought it was getting married. And now ... now I don't know what will make it better."

Caroline leaned across the counter, gripped the box of tissues, and pulled it toward us. I grabbed two and dabbed at my eyes, which had begun to sting. My head swam from the wine. I was a mess.

"Oh, honey," she started. "The problem isn't that you can't fix it. The problem is that you think it's broken. You think *you're* broken."

I *was* broken. At that moment, I was broken wide open. Every awful memory and moment spilled out, like the innards of a fish being gutted. I erupted in a wail.

I hadn't asked for my childhood. But it was all I knew. I had only known worthlessness. I had only known fear. And I had learned that the way to fight fear was by being tough. By being angry. By never letting them see you cry.

I believed in exercise not because I believed in health or beauty. I believed in *strength.*

Mighty Jo.

But all the kickboxing classes and elliptical laps couldn't change the fact that I couldn't help that little girl in me, or her mother, or her sisters. I couldn't rescue them. It further hit me that my being a drama magnet was about the challenge—let's see if Jo-Jo can get herself out of this jam. It was a test of strength, of will.

"I like Linus," I squeaked.

"Good."

"No, it's not. He likes someone else. Because I pushed him away."

"You had good reason," Caroline said. "It was so soon after Rex."

"I pushed Rex away, too. I push everyone away. But with Linus, I just ... I wanted to be *done*. I didn't want to ever make myself a target ever again."

"A target for what?"

I looked at her, confused. What did I mean?

Relationships were all about vulnerability.

Life was all about vulnerability.

Which was what had made Linus so attractive to me, I realized. He wasn't resilient because he was tough. He was resilient because he was vulnerable. Again and again.

And for the first time, I saw the error of my thinking: *Vulnerable* and *weak* were *not* the same thing.

"I see it so clearly now," I said. "I had never wanted to marry Rex. I just wanted to be what I thought was normal."

"You know what's normal?" said Caroline. "You going to pieces. Finally. You've needed to go to pieces your entire life. You've needed to allow yourself the courtesy."

"But then what happens?" I sounded and felt like a little kid trying to understand why the sky is blue. "What happens to the pieces?"

"You pick them up and put them back together. And if you do it right, you come out even more whole than before."

This sounded like greeting-card junk to me. Until I thought of Linus, taking a sledgehammer to that wall, the one he'd just put up. Regardless of why he tore it down, I knew he'd build a new one, and it would be better than the first.

Linus was all about the pieces.

Caroline the cop wrapped me in a most extraordinary hug. I cried on her shoulder for what felt like hours but couldn't have been more than a couple of minutes. I cried out my entire life, it seemed. Let out all the heartbreak, the disappointment, the abuse, the neglect, the struggle. She stroked my hair and back the way a mom would. I'd needed that, too. My pieces fell all over the place. And for once, it was OK. For once, I didn't feel like I'd been overpowered. It felt like something that had happened just in time.

HOURS AFTER CAROLINE LEFT, I lay in bed, Cholly's butt in my face and a tuft of her fur kneading in my left hand, and I replayed the night. Caroline was a good friend. The best. After she held me and gave me a glass of water and drew a bath for me, she still insisted we arm wrestle before she left. It's a thing we do. Come to think of it, it's a metaphor for the friendship we've built.

Caroline has never beaten me. Sometimes, she fares better than at others. But she never stops measuring herself against a standard—mine—that she's not certain she can reach. She knows the victory is in the striving. We're both that way.

Tonight, she won. I didn't have it in me. It's not that I let her win. Rather, it felt like I was allowed to let go.

It didn't feel like a beating. It didn't even feel like a failure.

When we met, Caroline had a husband and a little kid. She invited me in to break bread with them many times when we were both in college. As for me, I just wanted to get away from home. I didn't much care where. I remember being mesmerized by pictures of Monument Valley in Arizona when I was a kid, because it was so otherworldly that it literally represented Anywhere But Here. For a long time, when I pictured myself somewhere else, those iconic geological formations served as the backdrop of my mental image.

Eventually, though, away was just a university in a town I'd grown up in, just a couple of miles from the house where that growing-up had happened. Away was found in the classwork I enjoyed and dreaded, in bedrooms that weren't mine. I began to see my life in terms of thresholds: could I pass a literature course I didn't care about but needed to get my degree? Could I graduate with honors? Could I be the outstanding student in my business school? I didn't even really like business school, but I thought it could lead me to security, and that's something I craved. Once I was out in the working world, could I beat my performance goal? Could I double it? Triple it?

Years later, could I save the money necessary to buy my gym outright—no financing—as well as enough to live on while I brought it up to speed? Seemed impossible, but I did it.

I kept moving the goalposts. Testing my endurance. Building my strength. Even though I knew, in terms of exercise, how important rest and recovery was to strength training, I never applied it to my own life. Add more weight to the barbell. Increase the reps. Push, push, push.

It was time to rest and recover.

Before Caroline left, we talked about how the gifts of love and life that we need aren't provided by someone else, but by ourselves. Caroline came to that realization after her marriage just ended one day, seemingly without warning. Her husband walked in after work, said he was leaving, bang-bang, that's it, you're dead.

Except she wasn't. Not by a long shot. She fought back, she poured herself into her work and into raising her kid, and she demanded more of herself when less was coming her way. She picked up the pieces.

I'm not dead, either. Not by a long shot.

What do I want?

I want to be OK with whatever I want next.

I want to find a way to give it to myself.

And if I'm lucky enough—or maybe lucky isn't the word so much as blessed—to share those horizons with someone else, I want to be available to that moment, and all the rest to come.

It was time to pick up the pieces and put them back together.

Mr. Blue Sky

As Cheap Trick said, surrender

COUNSELING—you know, therapy, head-shrinking, whatever you want to call it—isn't my bailiwick. I'm more in the business of the gentle prod, the shouted warning. But I've accompanied your journeys enough to know what mental and emotional breakthroughs look like.

Jo-Jo Middlebury, this is a big day for you.

So much of human perception happens in a small window, the immediate field of vision, that small patch of life you can see in front of you. Jo-Jo has had more than the average amount of traffic in that window—not as much as some, but certainly more than most—from the earliest age. Survival came first. Love, when it showed up, came second. Nurturing? Almost none at all. And it shows, in every way you look at her. When Linus Travers cites her nonstop drama, he's not incorrect, but he's also not seeing the bigger picture, because he doesn't know the bigger picture.

Tonight, perhaps for the first time, Jo-Jo has surrendered what she can't control and embraced the unknown. She's finally realized that vulnerability isn't the enemy. She's about to face her ultimate test of strength, and it's ironically going to happen by her surrendering.

I've seen it throughout millennia, the way people crumble in the face of the unknown or the unanswered. It's not enough to want something and to have the time and place of the delivery remain mysteries. So many people want it all and want it now, and when they try to force it to happen, it all falls apart.

Jo-Jo has a chance at a different outcome, and I'm so completely excited for her because the possibilities are as wide as the ocean. No, really. They are.

I think I'll whisper as much into her ear. I always spook that dog when I do, but I think this time it's worth the stretch.

Easy, Cholly, easy. I'll just be a minute. That's a good girl …

Linus

I've made a mess

I'D FORGOTTEN TO FEED TOBY BEFORE I LEFT THE HOUSE WITH SARI.

The thought occurred to me a little before five a.m., when I awoke—it took me a second to remember I was at the Northern—and I couldn't get back to sleep. Sari snores. She said I do, too (Amanda always slept like a rock, thus I'd gotten no confirmation from her), so I wasn't in a position to chastise her.

I sat up straight, hopped out of bed, and tried to feel around for my boxers in the dark.

The snoring stopped and the sheets rustled. "What are you doing?" Sari asked, her voice faint and froggy.

"I have to feed Toby," I said.

"Where?"

"At home. My house."

She was more alert and assertive. "Now?"

"I completely forgot last night. Poor little guy hid under the bed after all the banging started and stayed there. I'm the worst cat dad ever."

"I'm sure he's still alive," she said, with more sarcasm than I was inclined to appreciate.

And then it hit me: *She thinks I'm bolting.*

Was I?

I stood up and turned on the light. We both squinted and blocked our eyes with our hands as if we were shielding the sun. "No. No-no-no-no," I said, rapid-fire, and climbed back on the bed. "I'm not doing a hit-and-run. I swear, it's all about the cat."

My gaze turned to her, under the sheet, enough showing to make me want to stay. Almost.

She peered at me, a look of worry taking over her face. "Are we OK, Linus? I'm really starting to have my doubts."

I should have confessed it all right there: *No, we're not OK. We jumped into this too quickly, did exactly what I said I didn't want to do. That's my fault, and it's my fault for letting it continue. We should end this now before we end it later.*

Instead, I caressed her cheek and pushed a strand of hair behind her ear. "We're fine. Last night was good. More than good. I'm glad we came here. We needed it."

"So stay," she beckoned, taking hold of my arm. "Don't go. I'm sure your cat will be OK for another couple of hours."

"I can't," I said. "I just can't. I'm sorry. I'll make it up to you."

How? Whisk her away to Glacier National Park? Yellowstone? Red Lodge? They were all socked in with snow, too. Maybe Chico Hot Springs.

"I don't want you to keep paying restitution," she said. "I just want you here. With me. And I don't just mean *here*," she said, rapping the bedsheet.

I kissed her even though we both had putrid morning breath.

"I am. I really am." And then, not knowing what else to say or do, I hopped up again. "We really have to go. Unless you want to stay here and I'll pick you up after I take care of Toby," I prattled, on the prowl for my boxers again, aware that if someone were awake and looking in the window from across the way, they'd just gotten an eyeful of my bare ass. There's an unflattering metaphor in there somewhere.

TOBY EMERGED THE MOMENT I OPENED THE DOOR AND CALLED FOR HIM. He gingerly stepped over and around the drywall, howling. I could practically translate it: *You bastard.*

"I know, I'm sorry, buddy," I said as I knelt to scratch his head. "I forgot. It won't ever happen again."

He wasn't having it. His distance and his gaze said, *Feed me, you inept piece of human worthlessness.*

I headed for the kitchen, grabbed his empty bowl—he'd licked it dry—and went to the cabinet where I kept his food, doling out a larger serving than usual, as well as quartering a slice of American cheese for him as appeasement. That cat loves his cheese. I held a mini-square out to him, and he took it away from my fingers as I felt a little nip. I refilled his water, set the bowls on the floor, and watched him munch voraciously.

I'd driven Sari and myself back to the house, and she went straight to her car. No kiss goodbye, no, "I'll call you." Just: "I don't know, Linus," right before she opened the door and slid out.

I promised to text her, but she was indifferent. Or maybe she didn't hear me. She was out of there so fast.

I deserved it. And I had no idea how to make it right, because deep down I knew I didn't want to. And that filled me with even more guilt and shame.

I looked around at the disaster area. My disassembled, lonely house. Certainly not a home.

Toby paused to look at me.

"It's all one big mess, Tobers," I said.

He dipped his head back into his bowl.

I was alone.

Jo-Jo

Spin cycle

LINUS AND I PULLED UP TO THE GYM SIMULTANEOUSLY AT 8 O'CLOCK AND waved to each other through iced auto windows. Regret dug into me again, same as it had for weeks now, as I realized anew that I'd never complimented him on how prompt he was until the one time he wasn't, and then I gave him heaping helpings of hell. I couldn't fix my life in one day, but this particular tendency—where I assume someone is going to do the wrong thing, so I come hard and fast with the punishment—needed to be addressed sooner rather than later. No time like the present.

We stepped out of our vehicles, and Linus toasted me with his insulated coffee mug.

"G'morning, Linus," I said. "Right on time, as usual." He smiled in an appreciative way, which made me feel good. "What's the good word?"

He shook his head. "I checked the shipment status. No change." For the fourth consecutive day, my computer system—the brains of the outfit, you could say—had stopped its forward motion on a shipping platform in Louisville. No amount of calling and pleading with the shippers had managed to spring it loose.

"So another day of waiting," I said. "Great."

"Well, no," Linus replied, walking a brisk line to the front door. "For me, there's the thrilling task of hooking up your laundry equipment. Gotta keep those towels fresh."

"I just hope I can eventually hand some out." It was a more sullen remark than I'd wanted to make.

Linus turned the deadbolt in the front door, then looked at me, holding my gaze.

"You will," he said. "It's going to happen."

His conviction was genuine. Not sucking up. Not positive for the sake of positivity, but honest-to-god we're-going-to-get-this-done-together. My heart began to rat-a-tat-tatter like a snare drum. It was downright magical to count on Linus. To count on anyone.

"Anyway," he added, "I'm glad you're here. I could use a friendly face today. Want to watch me play electrician?"

I grabbed the door handle and opened it for him, ushering him in. "I'd be riveted," I said, which elicited a chuckle from him, and a look of seeming surprise.

"That was funny," he said.

LINUS'S TASK, such as it was, couldn't have gone more smoothly. Within a half-hour, he successfully hooked my industrial washer-and-dryer set into the electrical system and the water/sewer lines, and for good measure he had a load of his work shirts and pants cycling through. You know, just to be sure.

"You've saved me a trip to the laundromat," he said.

"We aim to please at Mighty Jo's."

Linus gave my line the chuckle it deserved, and then he drew up a couple of folding chairs from against the wall and set them up so we could watch the spin cycle. He beckoned me to sit with him.

"I'm sorry about last night," he said. "It got weird."

I waved him off. "Don't be. Awkward situation. I get it."

"You have no idea."

I didn't think Linus was deliberately baiting me, but a line like that has one purpose: to elicit a "tell me more." But I didn't want to go there.

"Look, Linus, I appreciate your situation, and I'd love to learn how to be your friend—"

"You already are."

His matter-of-factness took me back. More than that, it was like a sledgehammer to the wall—*my* wall. For all the pushing away I'd done, for the lashing out, the mixed messages, everything, he'd already made up his mind.

I didn't have to "learn." I already was.

Wow.

It blew me away.

And yet, I still wanted more in the sense that I wanted to be a *good* friend, one with boundaries and not expectations. I wanted us to be confidants. Buddies.

But I also knew my limitations.

"What I mean to say is, I don't think I can talk to you about your relationship. I don't want to end up in the middle of anything or speak to something I'm not qualified to address. I used to do that with Larry, thinking I was being a friend to him, and I'm only just now seeing how much damage that might have caused. It's put our friendship in jeopardy, and I wouldn't want that to happen with you."

I braced for blowback. Expected him to pout and say, "Geez, I just wanted to blow off some steam, and you made it this big thing." But none of that came. He pursed his lips and looked at me and nodded, and then he turned back to the tumbling laundry and lost himself there for a few moments.

"That may be the wisest thing anybody's said to me in a long time," he said at last. "I'm guilty of the same thing on the other end of that relationship."

"With Jenn?"

"Yeah."

"How so?"

"Just what you said," Linus said, meeting my eyes again. "Jenn was actually Amanda's friend first—"

"Amanda?"

"My ex-wife."

"Oh, OK." Did I know Linus had an ex-wife? I thought Larry had said something, but I couldn't remember, and didn't really care. Now, something made me want to know more.

"Anyway," Linus continued, "Jenn really nurtured me through the pain of the divorce. I mean it. She was a real friend. And I leaned on her hard enough that I now come to find out resentment was building up in Larry. Something I never wanted."

"Apparently there were some land mines in their marriage," I said.

"No kidding," he replied.

The laundry cycle ended. Linus got up and transferred his clothes to the dryer, then started it up.

We sat and watched, transfixed. Odd how therapeutic that is. Meditative, even. To fix one's gaze on a shirt, a sock, anything, and watch it carelessly spin about. Like taking a cycling class where you're stationary, yet in motion. Not like you're not going anywhere. More like you're right where you need to be.

"So we definitely can't talk about me and Sari," he said, breaking the trance.

"I think that's for the best," I replied.

"I agree," he said. "Is there any law against us having a drink and talking about why we're so fucked up, in general?"

"Just the laws of time and space," I said. "The bars close at two a.m. I don't think we'll have enough time to cover the topic."

Linus broke into a wheezy laugh. "You're funny, Jo-Jo," he said again, as if it was a revelation.

I suddenly wanted to be funny Jo-Jo. Not snarky or sarcastic Jo-Jo, who makes jokes guised in passive-aggressive quips. But *funny*. Light-spirited. Good-natured. I wanted to make people laugh. I wanted to make *Linus* laugh. Hell, I wanted to make me laugh. How many times a day did I laugh? Not a snort or a chuckle, but an actual guffaw, a fall-over belly laugh?

Rarely, I realized. Yet another thing that needed to change.

WE LEFT THE GYM AT A LITTLE BEFORE ELEVEN IN THE MORNING. Having not yet reached the desperation of day drinking, Linus and I instead reconvened up the street at City Brew for coffee and analysis of our fuckupitude.

"Will you tell me about your marriage?" I asked once we were settled with our beverages and pastries.

"If you'll tell me about your almost-marriage," he said.

"Deal."

That's how I came to learn about the seven years Linus spent with Amanda, how cute little play fights turned into festering grudges, how at the end, as Linus told it, they were "two people living in the same house, playing out lives that rarely intersected."

"You think the end is going to be cataclysmic, some great confrontation, especially after seven years," he said. "But it wasn't. It was matter-of-fact. 'We're done here.' All the cataclysms were internal, as I unpacked every mistake I made, every uncharitable thing I said, every inconsideration I lobbed her way. The reckoning with myself was the worst part, because there's no hiding from it.

I had no responsibility for the ways she'd wrecked the marriage. I had complete responsibility for the ways I did."

For all the ways I'd crossed-examined Rex and me, I'd never thought of it in terms of *responsibility*. I doubt Rex ever did, either, if he was even capable of it. The realization that I needed to be responsible only for my feelings and behaviors was like a giant exhale. Yes, I always kept Rex at arm's length. And he treated me the way I had allowed him to. But his behavior? His actions? That was on him. I didn't make him leave me. He didn't have to call me a bitch. We had options. We could have *talked* about marriage, about what we wanted to be together, what we wanted for each other as well as from each other. And he could have said, *Hey, I'm afraid this isn't working* before he got up and walked out.

Over our second cup of coffee, I told Linus about New Year's Eve, hours before Larry and Jenn's party, and Rex's declaration that he couldn't allow himself to be tied down to a house or a town or a person. Or me.

"Good for you for dodging a bullet," Linus said.

"The one thing I did right was letting him go rather than begging him to stay. It's only now, in hindsight, that I realize he'd been telling me for a while, in indirect ways, who he was and what he wanted, or didn't want. I wish I'd seen it."

"I hear you. There was some of that with Amanda, for sure."

"Warning signs?"

"Red flags, yeah."

I looked over my coffee cup at him. "Why didn't you heed them?" Before he could answer, I caught myself. "I'm sorry. That sounded accusatory. I mean, with the benefit of hindsight, why do you think you didn't pay attention?"

Linus fixed me with that look-through-you gaze, something that for so long had unnerved me and now offered comfort, as if I could trust that I was being heard and considered.

"I've given this a lot of thought," he said. "I think it's a real simple, and real ugly, truth: I believed if I let Amanda get away, nobody else would ever want me."

I gripped my chair, feeling like some invisible force was about to knock me out of it.

He continued, oblivious. "Of course, what makes that thinking even more flawed is that Amanda clearly didn't want me, either."

I want you, I wanted to blurt out. But I couldn't. Not when someone else was already with him.

"Do you still believe that?" I asked, my voice suddenly quiet and mousy. "That no one would ever want you?" He leaned in closer to answer me. It was almost as if he was reading my mind.

"No," he said, although I couldn't get a read on whether he meant it. "Do *you* believe it, Jo-Jo? About you?"

I'd never doubted that Rex and wanted me. Or Larry at one time. Or even Linus. Or any other guy I'd dated. But did *I* want me? Would I ever allow anyone all the way in? Would I ever allow *me* all the way in?

My eyes welled up, and I looked down to hide them.

"*Wanting* isn't the problem," I said softly again. "It's *having*."

I was afraid to look up at him. Afraid to meet his eyes. But when I did, I saw compassion, empathy. Maybe even longing. And something unspoken between us. Like, *"You have more than you know."*

I invited Linus to move from coffee to lunch, but he said he had some things to do, including "finding a way to get those parcels off the shipping dock and on a plane." We parted in the City Brew parking lot with a wave, and I drove home.

CHOLLY GREETED ME AT THE DOOR WITH AN EASY SWISH OF THE TAIL AND nudge of the head that suggested mealtime was upon us. I fed and watered her, and brushed her coat as she happily crunch-munched her way through the kibble, and I eyed the kitchen sink and the mess strewn about the place. I'd been staying just ahead of my tasks since the start of the year, on through the slow procession of the gym's development, and I'd finally reached the end of my patience with it. I'd cleared stuff away several times, but now I aimed to go full-bore.

I brought out garbage bags and wet wipes, dusters and rags, and I set about a deep cleaning of my place. I'm talking the whole route: bathrooms, rugs, baseboards, behind the refrigerator. I wanted to get dirty, and I wanted my place clean.

An hour of industriousness was interrupted just once, and for good, when my phone pinged and I fetched it, reading the short text from Larry:

I left Jenn.

Linus

Fuckupitude

I DROVE HOME FROM CITY BREW REPLAYING NOT ONLY THE CONVERSATION over coffee but also the one Jo-Jo and I had while so casually watching my boxer shorts and flannel shirts and tube socks and jeans turning over in rote form, as if we were sitting in a bar and watching a ballgame.

It was really nice, actually. All of it.

I couldn't remember the last time I'd felt so comfortable sharing anything personal with anyone other than Jenn or my therapist. Even Sari and I didn't delve as much as we skimmed around the surface of topics regarding our exes and our dreams and our disappointments. And Jo-Jo stating clearly and respectfully that Sari was off-limits in terms of discussion ... well, let's just say I wondered if maybe Jenn should have done the same thing back when Amanda and I went belly up.

Or maybe I was in the wrong for not recognizing that a boundary should have been there in the first place.

You don't cross those lines unless there's a payoff. For me, it had been that while I was treading in the deep end of worthlessness, Jenn's repeated assurances that I had been too good for Amanda and not the other way around had kept me from sinking, to the point that I sometimes willingly jumped into that pool just to hear her say it. And that was a mistake.

And Jenn's payoff, I'm now realizing, was that she needed to feel her own sense of self-worth by being the life preserver.

Looking back, I remember how many times Jenn would say things like "Marriage is hard work," and she would say it with the exhaustion of someone who was subjected to prison labor without even a moment's reprieve. I once joked, "No one should have to work *that* hard," and I caught a look in her eye, one of equal parts discovery and sheer disappointment that at the time I couldn't decipher but now saw so clearly: Jenn had realized that she was working too hard. And the fact that she had to, that she was seemingly the only one doing so, and that perhaps that it had been futile, had crushed her.

I arrived home and was standing in the middle of my decimated living room, perusing the panorama to determine where to start cleaning up the mess I'd made, when the ring of my phone startled me. I simultaneously hoped and dreaded it was Sari.

It was Jenn.

Which was the proper response—answering it and hearing what she needed to say before honoring the agreement of not communicating, or enforcing the agreement by not answering at all?

I tapped the accept button on the phone's screen and spoke. "Hey, Jenn," I said, forcing the casualness.

"He left me, Linus," she said, followed by a sob and a sniffle.

My brain crapped out for a second. "Who did?"

"What do you mean, 'Who did?' My asshole husband, that's who."

It still took me a nanosecond to compute that she was talking about Larry. I'd never once thought of him as an asshole. Bryce? There was a bona fide asshole. But Larry?

"He *left* you?" I asked. *Geez, why was I so slow on the uptake?*

"For months I've been secretly praying for him to leave, or at least for something to happen that would shake us out of this pattern. I even thought about leaving myself, but, you know, Charlie. But I never thought he'd actually do it. And now that he has ..." She began crying again.

"I thought you had mutually agreed work on things first, then separate if necessary."

"We did. And then he went and shit all over that plan. Just packed a bag and said, 'I think it's for the best I leave right now.' Can you believe that? *I think it's for the best?* What about Charlie? Nice birthday gift to give the kid. Not to mention we had other social events coming up. Dinner with the Clineses, the church charity auction, my aunt and uncle's golden wedding anniversary ..."

"Shit, Jenn."

"You have no idea."

You have no idea.

I flashed back to just a few hours ago, when I'd uttered that exact phrase to Jo-Jo. I had always found it to be something akin to a rhetorical question, where you don't really expect an answer but imply that there is one. But I was suddenly cognizant of how loaded it was, and recalled that it was what had prompted Jo-Jo to put up her boundary then and there.

"Maybe we shouldn't be talking about this," I said, instantly regretting the bluntness of it. Jo-Jo's words had been careful, tactful, intentional. Mine? Not so much.

Jenn went on the defense. "Why not?"

I tried again, slower this time. "What I mean is, we had all agreed not to communicate for the time being, and I think it's important we honor that, as difficult as it may be."

She turned from defensive to outraged. "After all I did for you, this is how you repay me? By cutting me loose? What the f—"

"No, Jenn, that's not what I want. But my leaning on you so much was partly responsible for why Larry bailed on you. I know you're hurting, and believe me, I feel for you, especially since I've been stuck in that hole. But I can't jump in there with you."

"I jumped in there with you. Why can't you?"

"Because I have a girlfriend, for one thing."

This conversation was making me feel shittier by the minute.

"I had a husband. Didn't stop you."

Ouch. I felt the puncture in the middle of my chest.

"Precisely," I said. "Let's learn from that."

"Linus," she started. Desperation had seeped in. "I'm begging you. Please don't shut me out, too. I need you. I need you so badly."

I thought about that morning in the living room, when Larry accused Jenn of having romantic feelings for me. It didn't sink in then—I had refused to let it. It had been too uncomfortable. As if I had somehow unconsciously manipulated the whole thing. It still felt odd. Confusing. I had never looked at Jenn as anything other than the awesome mom and friend she was and is. But now I wondered: *What if this really was how all of this was meant to play out?* What if all these events had transpired in such a way that it was Jennifer, and neither Sari nor Jo-Jo, that I was meant to be with? What if the brass ring had been staring me in the face all along?

But it didn't *feel* like that. And what does *meant to be* mean, anyway?

Did I have an obligation to find out?

My phone alerted me to a text, and I caught a glimpse of it before it disappeared.

From Sari: *I don't think this is going to work out.*

The room spun. I reached for something to steady myself, and took hold of the exposed beam where the wall once was.

"Linus?" Jenn's voice was distant.

"I'm sorry," I said. "I just … I need time to process what you just said." I was referring to both Jenn and Sari.

"Linus, don't blow me off. Please."

"I'm not … this is all happening too fast. I just need me a little time and space. I'll call you as soon as I can."

I don't even remember if she said goodbye. Or if I did.

One second after I disconnected, the phone rang again, and I nearly dropped it. Geezus. I looked at the screen showing an out-of-state number.

"Hello?" I said weakly. Not my usual professional greeting.

"Hi, Mr. Travers. This is Hank from GymServ Software Systems. About Mighty Jo's computer system? We figured out why it got stuck in Kentucky. The mistake's on our end. We have it back here, and we'll get it to you by the middle of next week. Guaranteed this time. And the shipping's on us, plus a fifteen percent discount on the price. We're truly sorry for the delay."

Jenn's marriage was busting up.

Sari was gone.

Jo-Jo's gym would be finished in a week, and she'd be getting almost five hundred dollars back, which she badly needed.

I nearly burst into tears.

Jo-Jo

Fresh hell

WHEN LARRY'S TEXT CAME ACROSS, my first reaction was, "God, he's going to want to get together and talk about this," and I felt just awful about that. Of course he was. Who wouldn't want to talk to a friend in that situation?

But I didn't want that friend to be me. Not the way I'd always been. I knew how torn up and untethered he'd be, and the simple fact was that I no longer wanted to be the outlet for that. I wanted boundaries. I wanted to put an end to the drama once and for all.

So, of course, Larry rang my doorbell not five minutes after he texted me.

I wedged myself between the door and the frame, keeping Cholly at bay with my foot as she panted and danced about excitedly. Everybody was her friend. It must be great to be a dog.

"Larry, bad idea."

"Can I come in and talk?" he asked.

"Like I said, bad idea."

He didn't look good. Not surprising, of course, but it was even worse than I might have expected. His eyes were bloodshot, his hair splaying out in all directions like he'd just awoken, and he moved with a tension and twitch I'd never seen from him.

"This is bullshit, Jo-Jo," he said. "How many times have I been there for you when your life has been a shit pile? That's a lot, by the way. A lot of fucking times."

"You've been a good friend," I said. "And whether or not you realize it, I'm trying to be a good friend now." *Why was I so calm?*

"By kicking me out? What, you have a guy in there? Linus? Rex?"

There it was. *Now* he was starting to piss me off. *Kicking him out?* This wasn't his place, was never his place. It was as if he'd transplanted what had gone down with his wife onto our friendship. There's a word for that in the psychology lexicon, I'm sure. In any case, I was hell-bent on doing the right thing.

"I'm going to ignore that, too," I said. "And there's a time and place for us to talk, but not now and not here. I'm sorry about you and Jenn. Sorrier than I can even tell you. I think you should go find a place to sleep—"

"I was thinking here."

"No," I said. "No way."

"Jo-Jo, please."

"Get some rest, Larry. Deep rest. Then wake up tomorrow, and make a plan. Call me. I'll buy you lunch, dinner, whatever. We can talk then."

The nervous twitching had gone, replaced by something more melancholy, as if it was all being absorbed now. My heart ached for my friend.

"Jenn thinks I've always been in love with you," he said.

I sucked in a breath. "Is that what *you* think?"

"I think maybe she wasn't far off."

Oh, hell no.

"Larry—"

As quick and scary as a thunderclap, he was in my space there behind the door, ready to move in on me with a kiss. Just as quickly, I slammed the door on him, knocking him back on his ass as he grabbed his face, blood already spurting from his nostrils.

Cholly barked at the confrontation, no doubt as bewildered and hopped on adrenaline as Larry and I were.

Larry writhed, folding over at the middle. "Geezus."

I couldn't just leave him there. He might have had broken bones. Trembling, I opened the door and tried to help him to a kneeling position, but he reeled on his side, entrenched in the snow dotted with blood droplets, holding his nose as if to keep it from falling off.

"I'll get some ice for that," I said.

"Don't bother," he snarled.

"Look, I didn't mean to hurt you, but you were about to cross a huge line. Not just a we-can't-be-friends-anymore line. An I'm-pressing-charges line.

He rolled over and climbed to his knees. "I'm sorry. I'm just— oh, geezus."

I stepped toward him. "Are you OK?"

"No," he said, his voice still labored. "I'm beyond fucked up."

"Come on." I reached for him, slipping my hands under his arm and helping him to his feet. Step by small step, I walked him onto the sidewalk, toward his car.

He opened the door and lowered himself in, then pulled it closed. He leaned over to the backseat, pulled a T-shirt out of a duffel bag, and used it to wipe the blood from his nose, which was already turning a purplish-green. He couldn't look at me. I rapped the window, and after a few seconds of consideration, he lowered it. Tears marked his face.

"Call me tomorrow?" I said.

He raised the window, turned the key, and drove off.

You know when people say, "Hey, you look like you just lost your best friend"? Well, I didn't just look it. I did. I knew I did. What's more, I knew it was for the best. Didn't make me feel any better, though. I went back inside, plopped on the floor, and wrapped myself around Cholly until I cried it all out.

I WAS RECOVERING MY EQUILIBRIUM AFTER THE ENCOUNTER WITH LARRY when the phone rang.

Linus.

"What's up?" I said. Total affectation, that breezy opening. My heart was still doing rumbas in my chest.

"I just got off the phone with the computer vendor," he said.

"Oh, God." I braced myself for … well, just about anything.

"It'll be here next week," he said. "Total mistake on their part with the shipping. They're making it right. So you're coming out about five hundred bucks ahead, to boot."

"Next week?"

"Next week. 'Guaranteed,' the man said."

"Five hundred bucks?" That may not sound like a lot, but it's everything at this point. Everything.

"Five hundred smackeroos," Linus said. "Enough for cake and ice cream for everybody at your grand opening."

"You really have no idea what goes on at a gym, do you?"

"Aw, crap," Linus said. "I'm so stupid."

"Sometimes," I said with a laugh. "But mostly not. Anyway, today, you're my hero."

And then, right there on the phone, it all hit me at once. This moment I'd been waiting for, planning for, saving for—the only tangible thing I'd ever really wanted for myself in the world—was almost upon me. I cleared my voice on the phone to cover the emotion welling up in me and threatening to spill over.

"Thank you. It's been a hell of a day," Linus said.

"You have no idea."

He paused for a beat. "Do you want to go grab a beer?"

Mr. Blue Sky

Welcome to the human race

A VERY INTERESTING DYNAMIC IS PLAYING OUT HERE. Jo-Jo is getting emotionally healthy. She's responding more than reacting (well, except for merging her front door with Larry's nose; that was reflex, and justifiably so). She's learning what it means to be a friend, and what it means to accept friendship—heck, *anything*—from others, especially those she cares about. She's letting go and trusting, even just a little bit. And things are moving. They're unsticking.

Linus, on the other hand, is falling apart. And from my perspective, this isn't a bad thing. He needs this. He made great progress following his divorce, but his current predicament is signaling that there's more work to be done. What Jo-Jo is gaining, Linus is losing. That's precisely what happens sometimes. The human race is nothing but a hall of mirrors. You see someone, and how you respond to that person is largely determined by what he or she is reflecting to you.

Perhaps you see the qualities you want to develop in your own being. Or maybe you see the less-admirable qualities you know you have and are ashamed of. Maybe you see what you fear. Maybe you see the very best of you, or the very worst of you. The great guitarist Carlos Santana said, *"I am the reflection of the light within you, and you are the reflection of the light within me."* Some lights are dimmer than others. Others are brilliantly bright.

Now, let's talk Larry and Jennifer. Interesting what they're each projecting onto Jo-Jo and Linus, thinking these old friends of theirs are the water to fill their wells. Larry and Jennifer are mirroring lack. What they need to learn—what all four of them are in the midst of learning—is that only one person can fill the well.

And not with a soulmate. Or a fling. Or a best friend or a child or a dog or a cat or a gym.

I hear you, by the way: *Do something, Mr. Blue Sky! Don't just stand there angelsplaining all this to us. If you have the answers, then why don't you whisper it in their ears or something? Give them a sign. Plant a subliminal message. Make the Virgin Mary appear when they cut open an avocado.*

Have I not been here every step of the way? What do you think Linus taking a sledgehammer to his walls was all about? Not that I told him to do it. But he was cognizant of the discomfort and fear his life had become, and that was his reaction. And what might have happened had that computer system been delivered on time? Again, not me, but there was an opportunity for surrender and trust, and maybe I ever so gently assured Jo-Jo that she could while she slept.

So you see, I'm not in charge. The plan is this: you are all here to love one another as you love yourselves. You get my drift? I'm not talking about the ooey-gooey stuff. I'm talking Lou Grant's moment of *I treasure you people*. I'm talking about *the light*. And that's not all. This is part of the plan, too: *You get to choose* whether to accept or reject that light. You also get to choose whether to give or withhold that light.

And you get to ask for help. And then you get to choose whether to listen.

What's happening right now: This is the gift of the struggle.

If only you could see all of this through my lenses. It's dazzling. It's precisely this view that makes me able to do my job. And, friends, let me tell you: I love my job.

Linus

What's left undone

JO-JO AND I MET AT ANGRY HANKS. We each ordered a stout, and the we grabbed a table, our fingers taking turns plucking the popcorn in the basket between us. I noticed that Jo-Jo likes her popcorn with a little hot sauce on it. It says so much about her.

After clinking our glasses in celebration of the computer system victory and each of us taking a swig, we set them down and locked our eyes in a gaze, as if to say, *Where do we even start?*

Jo-Jo broke the ice. "I got a crazy-ass text from Larry today, followed by a visit."

I jumped in, "Oh god, me too—from Jenn! Not a visit, but a phone call. What the eff?"

"So messed up."

"It's kind of unnerving, if you ask me. I mean, if Larry and Jenn can't make it ..."

"Turns out they're human, Linus," Jo-Jo said before popping another few kernels, followed by a swallow of beer. She must have seen me wince, because she elaborated. "I didn't mean that to be snarky or cynical. I just mean ... I think we thought they were invincible, impervious to the stuff we dumped on them. We didn't take responsibility."

She was right, of course. And it's not like I didn't know it. But her statement was still sobering.

"What did Larry say?" I asked.

"Not much. I didn't really give him the chance. He was in no condition to talk rationally about anything." Her eyes became dark, as if she'd gone to another place in her mind.

"Same here. Jenn thinks ... well, she thinks she and I should be together."

Jo-Jo sat up straight. Thinking she was about to reprimand me, I interjected. "I'm sorry. You don't want to talk about my relationships." I sipped my beer.

"Well, considering Larry let on that he thinks maybe he and I should be together, I kinda think we should talk about this."

I nearly did a spit take.

"He *what*?"

She didn't repeat herself. She didn't need to.

I stared into the crowd, focusing on nothing and no one in particular. Jo-Jo's admission bothered me on multiple levels—that Larry had feelings for someone other than Jenn (as much as Jenn having feelings for someone other than Larry); that the someone was Jo-Jo (and that Jenn's someone was me); that maybe some cosmic romantic wires got crossed among the four of us.

"Do you think he's right?" I asked.

Jo-Jo looked startled. "No." She paused for a beat, and asked, "Why would you think such a thing?" Her tone was curious.

"Well, I know the two of you dated a long time ago."

"Another lifetime ago," she corrected.

"But there's still history there. And there was enough of something for you to remain friends all these years. I don't know, I'm just wondering what it all means."

"You think you and Jenn are meant to be?"

I tried again to picture it. Pictured myself in the Morelli kitchen, only it was Jenn's and my kitchen—having dinner and asking Charlie about his day, making plans for the weekend, doing the dishes together—and stopped short when an image of Jenn naked in bed formed and I felt icky, as if I'd just seen something I wasn't supposed to.

"No," I said definitively.

I took another swig of beer.

"What does *meant to be* even mean?" I asked. "Does that mean someone's pulling the strings, determining who gets paired up with whom? Or is it some lie that the movies made up?"

"I've always thought the latter, although I'm starting to think that's a rather jaded way to approach life on this mortal coil," Jo-Jo said. "That said, I don't believe in the man behind the curtain, either, if you know what I mean."

"I used to believe in romance," I said.

"And?"

"And now I don't."

"Me, either," she said.

I never heard anything so sad. "I would like to again," I offered.

She sat silent for a moment. Finally: "I would, too."

I saw something in her when she said it. The words came out softly and gently, so contrary to the toughness and hard edges that contoured her beauty.

And then I realized: for a split-second, she'd made herself vulnerable. Like a freshwater lake I wanted to dive into headfirst.

"What about Sari?" she asked, which snapped me out of the

moment, and then saddened me. I'd tried to call Sari earlier in the day, but the call went straight to voicemail.

"I thought—"

"I know, I put up a boundary when I said I don't want to talk about your relationship, and here I am stepping right over it. I'm sorry. But since we were just speculating on Larry and Jennifer, I guess I'm wondering where she fits in."

"I don't know that she does," I said, taking a more forceful pull of beer.

Its effects instantly rushed to my head.

Jo-Jo noticed immediately. "Everything OK?" she asked.

I shook my head, more in that exasperated kind of way, like wishing the merry-go-round would stop spinning. All I'd wanted for the New Year was a relationship. I didn't want my life upended. I'd had enough of that. I certainly didn't want the lives of my friends upended. I didn't want a relationship at their expense. And Jo-Jo … this stunning, assertive, determined woman, who it turns out is funny and has a soft side, was at the center of it all.

She was too much for me. All of it was too much.

And then suddenly I felt as if I had just opened my eyes, as if to discover I had been sleepwalking.

"I shouldn't be here," I said.

"We're just having a beer, Linus," she said. "At your invitation."

"I know. But I think I need to see Sari."

I stood up. Jammed my hand in my pocket to pull out my keys, when Jo-Jo leaned forward and took hold of my arm.

"Linus, don't."

"Don't what?"

"Don't do whatever it is you're about to do."

"Why not?" I didn't even know what I was going to do.

"Because you've got the same look in your eyes that Larry had when he came over. You're not thinking. You're just reacting to something that's got you feeling uncomfortable. I know that feeling. I usually don't react as much as I retreat or set my phasers on 'kill,' which isn't much better. But you've got to go home and take a deep breath and think things through, or sleep on them."

"You've been to my home. It's not conducive to thinking these days."

"Maybe there's a reason for that."

Clarity flooded in. All this time I'd been wondering what had gotten into me, why I had so maniacally taken apart all I had so meticulously built. *I had created my own chaos.* But for what purpose? What had I been trying to avoid or undo? More to the point, why had I bought a fixer-upper in the first place? It wasn't only to practice my mad skills, as the kids used to say.

"I'm pretty sure Sari wants to break up with me," I said.

Jo-Jo gave me a strange stare, as if she were deliberating on whether to continue the conversation or walk out on me. "What do *you* want?" she asked.

The answer rushed at me the same way the alcohol had. *I want you, Jo-Jo. Forever.*

And then I broke into a sweat and my pulse raced as terror crashed down on me like a tidal wave. *No. Not Jo-Jo. Anyone but Jo-Jo.*

I want love. I want romance. I want to believe in romance again. I want it to be easy this time. I want it to be real.

I want …

I just want to let go.

I sat down to steady myself and let the feeling pass, taking a few deep breaths. I could hear Jo-Jo beckoning: "You OK, Linus? Linus?"

I took in and blew out a hard, heavy breath, shaking off some of the panic, and sat down again. "Yeah, I'm OK now. This is quite a stout."

"You kind of scared me just now."

Me, too.

"I'm sorry, I just got woozy for a second."

"More than a second."

I could hardly form a thought, much less hold one. "Can we go outside for some air? I know it's frigid out there, but I'm baking in here."

We both stood up, and she linked her arm into mine to steady me as we made our way through the after-work crowd to the door. My heartbeat pounded like a bass drum. Her scent stood out among the competing smells of beer and popcorn and people. I liked the way our arms linked. As if they fit together.

Which, of course, made everything worse.

Outside, I leaned against the truck, feeling the ground underneath me, appreciating its firmness as I regained my equilibrium. My head cleared. My pulse slowed down. My body cooled off.

"I'm sorry, I said. "I'd wanted this to be an enjoyable night out. Shake off the day. Celebrate the win."

"I shouldn't have brought up Larry and Jenn," she said.

"And I shouldn't have mentioned Sari," I replied.

"I should have respected that boundary by not bringing her up in the first place," she volleyed back.

"And I should have ..." my lob hit the net. "Not drank on an empty stomach, I guess."

"Well, yeah. That was a pretty dumbass thing to do."

I chuckled, and the weight that had landed on my chest in the bar released itself, allowing me to breathe again.

"I guess I should go find something more substantial than popcorn."

"Bread," Jo-Jo said. "Lots of bread. It will absorb the alcohol. Go get yourself some fixings for a hoagie, too. And then get some sleep. It'll be better in the morning."

"You think so?" I asked.

She took a step forward, and before I knew what was happening, she wrapped me in an embrace. In that moment, I was grounded. I wanted to stay there forever. But she let go, and then put her gloved hand on my shoulder, which anchored me even more.

"You're a good man, Linus Travers."

No compliment ever dug in so deep. But why did she say it? What did it mean? Should I ask her? My head started to swim again, and when she removed her hand, I gently took hold of her arms to steady myself once more, my thumbs smoothing the satiny finish of her puffy coat. I could lean on her, and she could hold me up. "And you, Jo-Jo Middlebury, are a gem," I said.

She averted her eyes.

Feeling deflated, I removed my hand and turned to the door of my truck. "Thanks for talking me off the ledge."

"What are friends for?"

I wondered if she said that as a reminder to what we were and always would be. I could live in a world where Jo-Jo Middlebury was my friend and nothing more. Better than living in a world without her.

Then again, maybe that had been Larry's rationale, and look where it got him.

I had to lean on *me*, I realized. I was so good at being everyone else's buddy. I had to be a friend to me.

BACK HOME WITH A BLT FROM SUB COMMANDER, I ate about a quarter of the sandwich before feeling woozy again—seriously, I didn't even have that much beer—and retreated to the bedroom. Toby, already nestled in his spot beside my pillow, looked up at me before putting his head back down.

"Hey, buddy," I said. I held my fingers to his nose. He sniffed, and then licked the traces of mayonnaise from them before lackadaisically lowering his head on top of his front paws. I undressed and climbed into bed, not even bothering to brush my teeth, propped up the pillows, and closed my eyes.

In my mind's eye, all I could see was the rest of the house—the unfinished kitchen, the mess in the main room, the second bedroom neglected—could *feel* it all sloshing inside my skull. My heart started to race again. I opened my eyes and turned on a light.

"What do you say, Tobester—should we find a you-friendly hotel and sleep there for a few days?"

Toby meowed his disapproval and repositioned himself on the bed.

"It was just a suggestion. Geez."

I turned out the light and closed my eyes again. This time I heard Jo-Jo's voice: *Take a few deep breaths, Linus. Rest. Sleep on it. It will be better in the morning.*

I did just that.

When I awoke, sunlight streamed through the window so brightly you'd think it was springtime. And sure enough, I knew exactly what I wanted to do, what I wanted to say, and to whom. And I smiled.

Jo-Jo

Making it manifest

LAST FALL, when Rockin' Robiskey was still my contractor and I still had the naïve hope that my gym would be finished and open by the new year, I hired someone named Denise to help me build a webpage. Denise was great—a kid, really, just out of college, making it on her own as a developer, a real can-do sort of attitude, purple hair, a zippy way of talking that eluded me most of the time, but the point is she gave me exactly what I wanted: a Mighty Jo's Gym website with great tools for sustaining my eventual business.

For months now, all the great content Denise and I built— the backstory, the online membership submission and renewal, the class schedules, the personal-fitness tools—has lain in online purgatory, waiting for the gym to open. From time to time, I've tweaked something, like the projected opening date (most recent amendment: "sometime before Mighty Jo dies"). Mostly, though, I've left it alone as my hopes have darkened.

Now, Linus says we're a week away. I believe him.

Tonight, using the templates Denise gave me, I built a new page, one that will go live with the rest of the site in just a few days. I headlined it "Our Partner." And I wrote:

> *Mighty Jo's Gym would not exist without the kindness, patience, and tenacity of Linus Travers, owner of Travers Contracting of Billings, Montana.*
>
> *We could say that Linus installed the flooring and the lights, did the tilework and the plumbing, moved in and installed the exercise equipment, finished the walls, set up the computer system, and did all of it on time and on budget, and we would be entirely correct. We would also be leaving out the most important parts.*
>
> *When we didn't believe, Linus did.*
>
> *When we were sure we couldn't endure another delay or bit of bad news, Linus showed us how to adjust, recover, and push on.*
>
> *When we needed a friend, Linus was there.*
>
> *Any contractor can quote you a bid. Most of them can do the work. Some of them can even come in at or under budget.*
>
> *Linus Travers was as good as his word, start to finish. In our experience, that's a rare thing, indeed.*
>
> *We will never be able to thank him properly. We'll do our best by serving you as well as we possibly can, so what he built remains a part of the community for a long time to come.*
>
> *If you have a contracting job, no matter how small, call Linus Travers. Tell him we sent you. And prepare to have your dreams fulfilled.*

I anchored the page with a picture of Linus from his own website since I didn't have any of my own, and I suddenly wished I did. How many times did I watch him at work, the way he was always pushing his safety glasses up the bridge of his nose before he did heavy lifting, and when he leaned into the job he would wag his tongue out his mouth and off to one side, just a little bit. It made him look like a panting dog.

A *cute* panting dog.

So there Linus was, on my computer screen, minus the floppy tongue and sweat beading up on his forehead and his safety glasses slipping down his nose. Right above those words I worked so diligently to choose and arrange in the right order.

I reached down and found Cholly's waiting head, and I stroked it with my fingers.

"We have a good friend, girl," I said.

Not that I didn't want him to be more than a friend. But at the same time, having Linus as a friend felt calm and right in a way being friends with Larry never did. Turned out that I had mistaken "reliable" for "grounded." And not the good kind of reliable. I mean I'd leaned on Larry for all the wrong reasons, took for granted that he'd be there, maybe even took advantage. More and more, being around Linus was like a kind of knowing I'd never felt before. Maybe that's what people meant when they said something felt like "home" to them. I'd never had sense of home as anything other something chaotic and uncertain.

Then again, maybe I was also starting to feel like home because of *me*.

I PUT IN MY TIME ON THE ELLIPTICAL AFTER THAT, fueled not by angst and frustration but by elation, my pace getting away from me and my heart rate soaring beyond where I wanted it. I tamped down my energies and made it through my hour, and then I took a shower and tumbled into bed. Cholly dragged herself up onto the bed, and we were all set. I felt content.

We tried to watch a favorite old movie of mine, *Three Days of the Condor*, that I'd saved to the DVR months earlier. (Side note: I despise the whole "let's rate men" thing, because it engages in a kind of objectification that pisses me off when it's men rating women, but just this once, I'll give it a go. With regard to celebrities, I'll take early-1970s Robert Redford and you can have everybody else, OK?) As the film played out, I couldn't help but wonder where Linus was, what he was doing, if he liked movies in bed, if he'd like this movie, if he'd like this bed …

For the first time, instead of shutting myself down, instead of chiding myself, telling myself it was a waste of time, that I couldn't have everything I wanted just because I wanted it, instead of being what I would have called "strong," I allowed myself the courtesy of leaning in. I let myself want him. Miss him. Crave him. And funny how, when I did something so simple as to let myself have a moment of vulnerability, the feelings freed me.

I'd just about gotten myself off to sleep when my phone pinged, and a message came up from a number with a 406 area code, a number I didn't recognize.

Jo-Jo, it's Jenn. Can I call you?

I sucked in a breath. Holy shit. How to respond to this?

Be truthful, I decided. *I honestly don't know*, I wrote back.

I waited. The bubble quote with the ellipsis appeared on my screen.

I understand. If it makes any difference, I'm not angry. This isn't a takedown. I really do need to talk, if you can.

Dammit. Jenn was hurting. I could be sure of that, and I didn't want to leave her hanging. It was easier to slough her off by assuming she wanted a confrontation. To say no to need would just make me a jerk, and I didn't want to be that.

I'll wait for your call, I wrote.

I held the phone in front of my face, and I did what I said I'd do. I waited. And Jenn called.

Linus

It's all for the best. Right?

I SENT SARI A BOUQUET OF FLOWERS—not too romantic, not too Mother's Day—with a card attached: *One more dinner, please?* With nothing more to do at Mighty Jo's until the computer system arrived, I went back to work on my house, starting over, cleaning up, making a plan to get the entire job finished by the end of spring. Shortly after two o'clock, around the time the flowers would have been delivered, I received a text from Sari: *When and where?*

I smiled and typed, *Stacked. Where it all began. 5:30 tonight. OK?*

She responded with a thumb's-up emoji.

SARI WAS TEN MINUTES LATE—a long ten minutes—and by minute six of my wait I thought it was a reasonable possibility that she'd changed her mind and wasn't going to show, although I believed she would at least text me. She whisked the door open and entered with a whoosh, and I stood up to greet her. She apologized, and I helped her take off her coat. We didn't exchange kisses or hugs.

"Had to get my son taken care of before coming over," she said.

I liked her son. Kaden. Met him a couple of times. Good at math. Really good at computers. Dug board games, too. He and Charlie would hit it off.

"I'm sorry, I didn't even think about it when I invited you for tonight," I said.

She waved a hand. "No worries. I think he likes the occasional change-up. He's with a friend, so it's all good."

"I'm glad," I said. "And I appreciate your meeting me."

"I almost didn't," she started. Our server swung by, and she ordered a drink. "Thank you for the flowers. Not that they were what swayed me. But it was thoughtful."

"What did sway you?"

"You're a good guy, Linus. Nothing is going to change that. You don't deserve to get dumped and forgotten. And I figured we could both use the closure, although, man, I hate that word."

I hadn't thought of our situation as her dumping me, but the word sucker-punched me nonetheless. As for closure, I flushed with the realization that I craved it, in all things. I'd sought it too fiercely with Amanda at the end, and I remembered my therapist telling me that closure was overrated. "Some things just end," she'd said. Here I was again.

"Me, too," I lied. "Although that's kind of why I asked you out tonight. I feel the need to explain why things didn't work out."

I had expected her to be nervous, guarded. But she seemed calm and ready, especially after her cocktail arrived and she took a sip. "Go ahead."

"Remember what we talked about on our first date in terms of what we wanted?"

She nodded. "You wanted friendship. I wanted fun."

"Well, I should have listened to myself and not jumped into bed so soon," I said, leaning in and speaking slightly above a whisper, especially the words "into bed." "Although I really liked it."

"So did I," she said, leaning in as well.

"And I like you. You're just so great."

She chortled and picked up her drink. "Buuuuut ..." she drew out before taking another sip.

"I wanted more. And I got more. I just got it in the wrong order. I wanted to get to know you and spend time with you and cook meals and things like that with you *before* we did the other thing, not during or after."

"It was all supposed to be good fun, Linus," she said. "Sex doesn't have to be serious. It doesn't have to be commitments and making room in the medicine cabinet. We were just dating, you know?"

"It's serious to me," I said. I'd never admitted that to anyone before. Heck, I'd never admitted it to *me*. "I guess I'm hardwired that way. Which is precisely why I wanted to give it more consideration."

She looked at me as if we were at an impasse. "I really like you, too, Linus. I think you're equally great. And funny, and cute, and good in bed. But I think you want something I can't give you, whereas I just want to enjoy the relationship for what it is and not really work on it. I'm done working for my relationships."

I was curious what she meant by that, wondering if she'd gone through her marriage the same way Jennifer went through hers, the same way I'd gone through mine, trying to make it be something each of us feared it wasn't. Trying to be someone we each feared we weren't. Sari talked so little about her marriage and divorce. Never had a bad word to say about her ex or her marriage, other than "it was for the best" that it was over, and she finally wished him well. I wondered what she felt before "finally," if she struggled to let go, or forgive him, or maybe forgive herself. I had never asked her, and those were the things I'd wanted to know, like the way Jo-Jo and I had opened up to each other. The way Jenn and I talked so many times.

I wasn't going to ask her now. And I couldn't help but compare her with Jo-Jo, who in the past week seemed to be finally opening up. Where Jo-Jo was hard around the edges, Sari was soft. Where Jo-Jo was reserved, Sari was forthcoming. Where Jo-Jo was driven, Sari was carefree. I couldn't see one stepping into the other's shoes, nor would I like one more than the other had they traded personality traits. I liked each one for who she was. But I also realized that Sari had closed a part of herself off, too.

"So where does that leave us?" Sari asked.

"I'm not sure," I said. "I'd like to see you. I just don't want ... at least not for the time being, even though it was really enjoyable. But I don't know if we can go backward after we ..."

She laughed. "Did you teach in a Catholic school or something? You can say the word *sex* in public. No one's within earshot of us. And even if they were, what's the big deal? It's *sex*," she said, a little louder and even more emphatically, laughing mischievously again. I winced, thinking she was right. What *was* the big deal?

I laughed amiably. "I was a high school teacher. You didn't dare utter the word in front of a bunch of horny teenagers, especially boys."

"Point taken."

"Anyway ..." I continued. "Would you still want me in your life?"

"I would. But Linus, I liked the sex."

"I did, too."

"I don't know that I want to part with it."

"Can't we try?"

Sari squinted her eyes, as if trying to see me a little better. "Do you even know what you really want?"

Last night, following the woozy encounter at the bar, the answer to that question had been crystal clear. And hadn't I been saying it all along? *I want romance.*

"I'm glad I met you, and I want to continue getting to know you," I said. "But I also know I want to build a relationship from the ground up. Lay down a foundation of friendship. Put in the sub-floor by getting to know what makes you vulnerable, and vice-versa. You can be vulnerable when you're just friends."

She peered even closer. "You sure you're a guy?" she said, and laughed yet again.

Now I was irked. "Why can't a guy want a serious relationship? Why does he have to be suspect?"

"Well, you have to admit, it's weird."

"It's not weird. And it's not fair. You're emasculating me just because I want something that doesn't include Bud Light and a box of Trojans. And maybe more guys would be willing to try it if they'd stopped emulating those stupid beer commercials."

Contrition crossed her face. "You're right. I'm sorry. I shouldn't have made fun."

I barely heard her apology, still feeling the sting. "I'm trying to come clean with you, Sari. I haven't been honest with you these past few weeks, or with myself. I know what I want, and I'm communicating it to you, or at least trying to."

"Maybe it would be for the best if we just let this go," she said. "Maybe down the line we can be friends. But right now, it's just not what I want. I don't want what's between us to be any more or any less than what it was. I'm sorry. Maybe we just see things differently, and that's OK."

This was not how I'd wanted this to go. I had woken up this morning thinking we were going to have another go. I had thought that if I'd established better boundaries, 'fessed up, and clearly articulated my intentions, Sari and I would be on the same page for a new starting point. It hadn't occurred to me that doing so would only shed light on how far apart our intentions were, that we *couldn't* get on the same page. Or didn't want to. And here I heard my therapist's voice again: "Some relationships are cab rides. They have a beginning and an end." I hadn't anticipated that, and now I felt stupid. I should have been ready for this.

Our food arrived, and my appetite was gone. Sari's was, too, I surmised, from the way she sort of just looked blankly at the plate without touching her silverware. We sat in uncomfortable silence despite the bustle and chatter of the restaurant for what seemed like minutes but was probably no more than a few seconds. Sari called the server over.

"Can I get this to go?" she asked. The server nodded. I turned crimson.

"And for you?" the server asked me.

"Please," I said. I felt dejected. And even though no one seemed to even know we were there, I felt as if all eyes were on me. Watching me being dumped. Because that's exactly what it felt like.

Sari looked at me. "I'm sorry," she said again.

"Me, too."

She reached across the table and took my hand. "No, Linus, I really, really am. I want more for you. I want you to have what you want. But we both know that I can't give it to you."

"Will you come to the grand opening of Mighty Jo's gym next week?" I asked, practically begged. "Please? I worked so hard on it, and I want you to see what I do. It would mean so much to me."

The server returned with two Styrofoam to-go boxes and the bill. I handed her a credit card.

"I'll think about it," she said. And then, a few beats later, she added, "I should pay for my meal."

I shook my head. "I invited you."

"But—"

"It's my treat, Sari," I unintentionally snapped.

She turned cold. "Thank you." With that she boxed her dinner, said goodbye, and left the restaurant.

So much for closure. Although I hadn't actually wanted closure. I had wanted a reset, a fresh start.

Maybe I was getting one. Maybe this was what my counselor meant when she told me "Sometimes, the best you can do is figure out what is for you, and what's not."

I'm trying.

Jo-Jo

Loose ends

YOU KNOW THOSE HOLIDAY STORIES WHERE IT'S ALL ABOUT THE ANTICIPATION, counting down the days and placing all your attention on that one gift you've been wanting, have been asking for since July? Think *A Christmas Story*. All that hoping. All that emotional energy spent on a desire that seems both accessible and the longest of longshots.

That's what it was like, waiting for the computer system to come in. Linus checked in with me every day, usually by text, and assured me everything was on track. Meanwhile, I filled my time by adding content to my website, building ads for the Mighty Jo's Facebook page, setting up a mailing list, and long runs both on my elliptical and outside. Snow was melting faster than it was coming down, as if springtime were just as anxious for my gym to open as I was.

Though I'd asked Larry to call me after I literally slammed the door on him, he waited three days, and he didn't call. He texted.

Hate me?

I typed: *Of course not. You ready to talk?*

Yeah. Usual place? Fifteen minutes?

I was pleased to see the suggestion, as if we were stretching out toward normalcy.

I'll see you there, I typed.

SEEING LARRY AT CITY BREW ON 27TH WAS MUCH LIKE IT HAD BEEN A few days earlier, when I was looking at a haggard, sleep-deprived version of my friend. We didn't hug or shake hands. We just sort of sat and stared and mumbled about the weather. And then Larry, in small bursts and then larger ones, gradually came back to me.

"I was a dick," he said.

"Yes, you were."

"I'm sorry."

"You're forgiven."

"I feel like I need to—"

I stopped him. "Larry. You're forgiven. Seriously. There's nothing you could say that would heighten my understanding of it, and there's nothing I can say that will more thoroughly absolve you. The end."

He breathed a sigh of relief. "Thank you."

"Where are you staying?" I asked.

"The Best Western. Close to work. Close to restaurants. But I'm not working—I took some of the paid time off I've been racking up for the last five years—and I'm eating from take-out boxes on the bed, watching bad cable TV. I think I'm falling in love with Chip Gaines."

I chortled and coffee spilled out of my nose.

"Laughter," he said with a faint smile. "Nice to hear."

I dabbed at my nose and mouth with a napkin. "So what's the plan?"

Larry got a faraway look. "Go home. Kiss my kid." Tears began welling in his eyes. "Do whatever needs to be done to fix this."

"Good plan, I'd say."

"But it's not a plan," Larry said. "It's a pipe dream."

"Yeah, but what if I told you it wasn't? What if I told you that I've been watching you and Jenn for a long time and marveling at your way with each other. Envying you, even, but only in the best way. Rex and I never had what you two have. You and I certainly didn't have it. We were good friends. But you and Jenn—"

"We're over. I get what you're saying, Jo, but we're way beyond that now."

"She doesn't think so."

His mouth dropped open. And so I revealed my phone chat with Jenn, but only because she'd asked me to. Not the entire conversation, but the part that mattered most.

"When you see Larry again—" Jenn had said.

"I honestly don't know if I will," I'd interjected.

"Well, then, if you do, tell him that I called you, that I'm not angry anymore, that I'm ready to work on this whenever he is. Tell him we have too much built to just walk away."

"I will," I'd said.

"And tell him I still love him," she'd added.

Other parts of the conversation revisited me, too:

"I'm sorry about accosting you at Brew Pub the way I did. Truth is, I've always been insanely jealous of you, Jo-Jo."

"Well, here's a newsflash for you, Jenn: I've been so envious of you I think my skin is a permanent shade of green."

She'd been stunned to hear this revelation. "Why me?" She'd asked.

"You have it all: A guy who loves you. A kid who needs you. A beautiful house and career and friends that you don't have to keep at arm's length. And you're pretty and smart and funny and all the things that makes Larry love you so much. And why Linus has leaned on you so hard."

She'd sobbed. "I thought he did. But he's never gotten over you."

"He's never gotten over the idea that he could save me," I'd said. "That doesn't make for a healthy relationship, friends or otherwise. You're the one for him, Jenn. And not because you need to be saved."

"I think I ruined things with Linus, too," she'd said.

"If there's anything I know about Linus—and I don't know nearly as much as you—it's that he's very big on second chances."

LOOKING DIRECTLY AT LARRY, I said, "She loves you, hoss."

I'd expected him to be uplifted and encouraged. Instead, he looked downright crestfallen.

"I can't," he said.

"Can't what?"

"Go home. I wouldn't even know where to start."

"You just said a minute ago that you were ready to go back, kiss your kid, and do whatever needs to be done to fix this. Your words."

"I said what I *want*, not what I was ready for."

"You are ready."

"I'm not."

"You are, you can, and you will." His hesitation was the same as what I'd seen in people who wanted to start living healthier but were too overwhelmed to know how or where to begin. You just begin. Exercise. See a doctor. Quit smoking. You do it for a day. Then another. Then another. You try and fail and try again. And it comes together because eventually your habits change.

Funny, I never thought you could do that when it came to your past or your feelings. I'd thought you just lived with the hand you were dealt.

"Larry," I added, "there's nothing more important than this."

"I can't describe it, Jo," he said. "I tell myself at night, I say, 'Just stop this. Reverse it. Go back.' And then I dig a deeper hole the next morning. I can't get out of it."

"I know that hole," I said. "I've been in it. Which means I also know there's a way out of it. As your friend, I know you can do this."

My phone pinged. I checked it under the table.

Computer system at UPS in Billings!!!! Delivery tomorrow!!! OMFG!!!!!!!!!

The room went loopy on me, like a Dali painting. I felt faint. I must have looked it, too.

"You OK?" Larry asked.

I gripped the edges of the table and steadied myself. *It's finally happening.*

"Yeah," I said.

"You scared me."

"I'm OK," I said, resolute. "Listen, Larry, I think you just need to start with a small step. How about coming to my grand opening next Friday?"

Mr. Blue Sky

Keep going

WHAT? Get out of here. I've got nothing for you.

I just manifested some Jiffy Pop and am settled in for the rest of the show.

Suggest you do the same.

Linus

Ain't it grand

I'VE NEVER HAD CHILDREN, so I don't know exactly what it's like when the day of your son's or daughter's birth finally arrives. But walking into Mighty Jo's gym, decked out with bunting and welcome balloons and dance club music booming through the sound system, greeted by smiling, newly hired staff members in uniforms, and seeing every wall and tile and light fixture in its place, taking notice of how the bright colors invited me to use the state-of-the-art equipment, and a spiffy computer system to sign me up for a membership ...

Well, I may have gotten a bit emotional. Jo-Jo's baby was born.

OK, I admit it: It felt like my baby, too.

At the main entrance sat a table full of raffle prizes consisting of gift baskets full of power bars and protein powders and water bottles, gift certificates for personal trainers, running shoes, and activewear, and a grand prize of a lifetime membership. I filled out two entry forms—one in Sari's name, and one in Jennifer's. Sari had never given me a firm answer to my invitation, but I remained hopeful.

I took in the panorama of the space—delightfully packed with prospective new members trying out the equipment, sampling free protein bars and smoothies, and taking a tour of the facilities. When I spotted Jo-Jo, my breath stopped.

She was sporting workout gear in neon colors, a T-shirt with Mighty Jo's name and logo, and her silky hair pulled back in a ponytail under a Mighty Jo's cap.

She was, indeed, Mighty Jo. Standing tall. Confident. Radiant. Powerful, yet also graceful.

But there was something else, too. Something softer. Calmer. More at peace.

I was awed by her, even more so than when she had so boldly stepped up to me, taken hold, and kissed me. Awed by her beauty. By her boldness. By her determination and passion.

I was in love with her.

I approached her. She was talking with some patrons who had just signed up, thanking them. When she saw me, she stopped talking.

Her eyes welled up.

And then my eyes welled up.

And then she excused herself and stepped toward me until we were face to face, and she threw her arms around me, and we held each other, both of us bawling. We were goddamn Jerry Maguire and Rod Tidwell.

"Thank you," she said, her voice muffled in my shirt. "Thank you for making this day possible."

"Thank you for letting me be a part of it," I said between sobs. We unlocked and stood apart. "The place looks fantastic. *You* look fantastic. This is all you, Jo-Jo."

"I couldn't have done it without you."

Our eyes locked into a glassy gaze, and I wanted to take her into my arms, kiss her until the sun set, and inhale her scent well into the night. She stood transfixed, as if she were reading my mind.

And then I heard a voice. "Linus?"

I turned around. *Sari.*

And several paces behind her was Jenn, who also made eye contact with me and smiled.

I didn't know whom to address first, and settled with a generic, overzealous "Hiiiii!"

To my surprise, Sari kissed me on the cheek, and I caught the pained expression on Jenn's face as she witnessed it. I felt an ache. I'd been separated from my friend, and I missed her.

"Well," I said, "you made it."

"I figured I owed it to you to be here. And I really did want to see your work—finished, that is," Sari said with a chuckle. I laughed as if she'd just said the funniest thing ever, when Jenn stepped up.

"Hi, Linus."

Beads of sweat formed at my temples. "Jenn!" I said as if she'd just appeared. "I'm so glad you're here. Thank you for coming." I moved in for a hug, and then thought better of it and pulled back. More aching. A hug used to be a given. I missed it. I missed when we were all friends.

"Jo-Jo invited me," she said.

"Really? Wow. That was ... that was nice of her. OK. Well, Jennifer, this is Sari, my ... um, my friend. And Sari, this is Jennifer, also my friend."

God, kill me now. Please. A blow to the head, a strike of lightning. Anything quick.

"You're the Jennifer who helped Linus get over his divorce," Sari said.

"I guess I am," Jenn replied.

"Thank you for doing that," Sari said.

"You're the woman Linus is dating," Jenn replied. I couldn't get a read on her tone, if she was jealous or passive-aggressive or simply stating a fact.

"Who wants an energy drink sample?" I asked.

"We're not dating anymore, but yeah," Sari said.

"There are some free protein bar samples, too," I added. "Mmmmmmm, chocolate! Organic, too."

Jenn looked at me, then at her. "Oh. I'm sorry, I didn't know."

"Have you seen the Pilates room?" I asked.

"We just got here," Sari said.

Just clock me with a kettle bell.

"That's true," I said, wiping the sweat from my forehead with my sleeve. "Want me to show you both around?"

Jenn looked momentarily distracted, and when I looked in the direction she had fixed her gaze, I saw why. Larry had just entered and was taking in the entire space, as if he'd never seen the inside of a gym before. I remembered looking at the Pictograph Caves just outside of Billings the same way when I was on a class field trip as a kid.

My heart thumped to the beat of the house music.

Larry spotted Jenn in the crowd, and he ambled toward us. He looked like shit, quite frankly.

I froze, thinking he was going to punch me.

"What are you doing here?" he asked Jenn before turning to me with a murderous look. "With *him*?"

"I am not *with* him," Jenn said. "I came here because Jo-Jo invited me."

Larry looked stunned. "She invited *you*?"

"Shocking, isn't it?" Jenn said.

"And yet, here you are, talking to your superhero," Larry said.

I felt myself turning crimson, my entire body now drenched from sweat.

Sari turned to me, and I noticed that she, too, wanted to bean me with a blunt object. "I'm going to leave now."

"Please don't." And now, unlike the last time I was in an awkward spot with her and I'd had the wherewithal not to utter the worst five words ever, my good senses abandoned me. "It's not what you think."

That's when Jo-Jo walked up, looked at all of us, and said simply, "Oh, good. You're all here."

Jo-Jo

My gym, my party

"BEFORE ANYONE SAYS ANYTHING ELSE"—I looked straight at Linus—
"or does anything he's going to regret a nanosecond later"—now my
gaze was on Larry—"or draws any conclusions she can't support
with the evidence"—I was on Jenn now, who locked right back in
on me—"or leaves without the full story"—I turned to Sari. She'd
kind of stepped into the middle of something here, but I wanted to
give her my trust and assurance. If she'd shown up to support Linus,
she was good by me. Sari, in return, offered me *her* trust, which
made me feel good. I went on. "Please allow me to say a few things.
It is my gym and my party after all. My day of jubilee."

After that preamble, I tried to walk back the gravity of the
situation. A few people—not many—sensed what was going on and
crept in for a closer look. I wanted them to go back to trying out the
equipment and sampling the energy drinks while I said my piece.

I motioned for Linus and Larry and Jenn and Sari to move into a tighter huddle.

"Here's the deal," I said. "This gym—seeing it to completion—has taught me something, a lesson I didn't realize I needed until it appeared. This didn't happen because of my willpower or drive—"

"Yes, Jo-Jo, it did," Linus said.

"No." I reclaimed the floor. "And shut up until I'm done." I wanted to laugh as I said it, so he wouldn't feel chastened, and instead I choked up.

"It happened," I continued, my voice breaking, "because I have a community. And I needed community. I always thought I needed to get through life on my own because I was the only one I could depend on. I was so completely wrong. Not only do I need one, but I *want* one. And that's you, Jennifer, and you, Larry, and even you, Sari, which may surprise you since we really don't know each other at all. You mean something to me because you mean something to Linus."

Now I turned to Linus, my eyes misty. "If Larry and Jennifer aren't together and aren't my friends, and they're not *your* friends, I never meet you, Linus. And if I don't meet you, I don't realize my dream of owning this gym. Period. End of story. It doesn't happen. I was going to pull the plug, but you asked me for a shot at it. So here we are. And today, when everything I've waited for and wanted was realized, the scariest part of that scenario is the part where I don't meet you. Because then I don't meet the best friend I've ever had."

I took one quick look at Linus, and he was about to do the ugly cry again. Frankly, I loved that about him. He was a man who wasn't afraid to cry, much less cry in public. Which was saying a lot, considering I couldn't stay there another minute lest *I* break into the ugly cry. I turned to Larry and Jennifer.

"You love each other," I said. "You've both told me so. How to fix it, I don't know. I just know it will be the biggest waste ever if you don't. Because I love you both."

The tears got loose again and spilled down my cheeks. We were all crying now, every one of us. Even Sari. Mushy, gooey tears that had been waiting for a long time to escape and had finally found their moment.

"This truly is a day of jubilee," I said. "Thank you for coming. Try the coconut balls."

I turned away from my friends and walked back into the throng of a one-time retail space, now expertly renovated into a state-of-the-art gym.

My gym. In my city. With my people.

AN HOUR OR SO LATER, I felt a tap on my shoulder. When I turned around, there was Linus.

"What's your name?" he asked.

I gave him that *are-you-on-dope* look of puzzlement.

He smiled mischievously. "Never mind. Doesn't matter."

And then, like one of those amnesia characters you see on TV, it all came back to me.

New Year's Eve.

Linus cupped my face in his hands, leaned in, and touched my lips with his. A sweet, warm—*romantic*—kiss. The kind that stops time. That aligns planets. That erases bad memories.

And when he was done, he grinned in satisfaction, said "OK," and walked away.

Just like that.

Mr. Blue Sky

I'm not crying—*YOU'RE CRYING!*

Linus

Resolutions

We had a lot to celebrate several months later when New Year's Eve arrived. In addition to a full year of Linus Travers Contracting under my belt, an interview I did with *The Gazette* was published that morning. The article, headlined *A Contractor and His Community*, announced my new business, South Side Flip, in which I would be buying, renovating, and selling houses on the South Side of Billings at affordable prices and contributing a share of what I made to community nonprofits. Based on the wild success of Jo-Jo's gym, I also received contracts to renovate several buildings for new businesses.

It was Jo-Jo who had given me the idea about the community work. When she wasn't at Mighty Jo's (she had hired competent management, including her friend Caroline the cop, who was ready for a career change, thus allowing Jo-Jo to ease up on the reins), she was at my place, helping me finish renovating my home in between the new jobs that had come to me. Together, we tore down and put up new walls, rehabilitated floors, refinished cabinets, installed an island, painted, decorated, and turned the once-neglected eyesore into a stylish home.

I was in the driveway on a sunny day in early September, the front door balanced on a couple of sawhorses while I gave it a coat of red paint. Jo-Jo was a few feet away, planting bushes and seeds for spring blossoming. She had cleaned the front steps and adorned it with a new welcome mat, overhead lights, and decorative gourds. We stood at the curb to admire the sight, our arms around each other, when she said, "A little love goes a long way, don't you think?"

I turned to her and caught the radiance of her skin and the sparkle in her eyes. One would think it was the sunlight's reflection, but I knew better.

"It does," I replied. We looked at the other houses nearby—paint chipping, lawns brown and patchy, missing roof shingles, and it occurred to me that mine now stuck out for different reasons. She gazed in the direction of the house she grew up in, and I could read her mind.

"It's not fair, is it?" I said. "They all deserve more."

She nodded, still in an otherworld.

"They deserve *you*," she said, and my heart swelled.

That's when she kissed me. Again. She always had perfect timing with kisses.

And that's when it came to me. I went to the bank the next day, applied for a loan and, using my own house as collateral (its value had increased by more than thirty thousand dollars), purchased a house right down the block from my own, one that had been abandoned in foreclosure.

So, back to New Year's Eve ...

We were all mingling in Larry and Jennifer's living room,

repainted and rearranged (a job I'd helped them do), when Jennifer produced the jar of everyone's resolutions from a year earlier, and read them aloud. Even though Jenn didn't reveal names (or maybe I had been the only dumbass to sign and time-stamp mine), it was easy to identify some people based on their cringing, while others outright copped to theirs, laughing as they boasted about not even making it through one month of exercise or not drinking. Others proudly celebrated their accomplishments of being smoke-free, debt-free, or home from their dream vacation.

"Next one," Jenn started, and she smiled softly. *"Fall completely, unequivocally, deliciously in love and be in a committed relationship."*

I blushed as some people snickered, while a couple of women let out an *awwwwwww*. It was hard to tell if people took notice of my face matching the color of the sangria or if I was self-conscious and projecting all eyes on me. Jo-Jo squeezed my hand.

"I wonder how that worked out," someone muttered.

It worked out really well, actually.

It happened gradually. Patiently. Like renovating a house. First, the foundation. Next, the walls. The wiring. The plumbing. The floors and the fixtures. The finishing touches. And then it's home.

IT HAD BEGUN THE MOMENT JO-JO ADDRESSED US AT HER GRAND OPENING. The intersection had had all the makings for a collision—triangles galore of Sari, Jenn, and me; Larry, Jenn, and me; Larry, Jenn, and Jo-Jo; Sari, Jo-Jo, and me. And it was Jo-Jo, once notorious for being a drama magnet, who defused the situation so calmly and skillfully that it left us all a little startled once we all stopped bawling. When Jo-Jo walked away, Larry turned to Jenn and looked in her eyes, seeing the pain he'd caused her as well as the reflection of his own inner turmoil, and he pleaded, in a voice that matched Charlie's, "Can I come home?"

Jenn, sobbing, wrapped her arms around him. When they

released each other from their embrace, Jenn took his hand and they left the gym.

That left Sari and me.

I wiped my eyes with the back of my hand. Sari extracted a packet of tissues from her purse and handed one to me after taking one for herself. We blew our noses, and she gingerly dabbed at her eyes, erasing the rings of mascara that had formed underneath her lower lashes.

"Well," she started, "I've never had *that* reaction at a gym before."

"Neither have I."

"I'd still like to look around."

"I'll show you," I said, and I linked my arm into hers. Every nook and cranny had a story to tell—before and after, failure and success, then and now—and I relayed each one. I practically knew my way around blindfolded. I revered everything about the space. I'd given it all of me. And yet, everywhere I turned, I saw and heard and smelled and felt Jo-Jo.

"You did an incredible job, Linus," Sari said. "You have every right to be proud. I'm proud of you, too."

"Thank you," I said. "That means a lot to me, especially coming from you."

We returned to the lobby and went to the table with the samples. I handed her a mini-cup containing a chunk of a protein snack bar, along with a small bottle of water. We touched our cups together in a toast and popped the samples into our mouths. Then our eyes connected, knowing the words that were about to follow.

"You're in love with her," Sari said.

I gulped. "Who?"

"Jo-Jo. I knew it the moment I saw the two of you together at your house. That's why I reacted the way I did that night. I was disappointed."

The protein bar sat in my throat. Or maybe it was just the truth.

"I'm sorry," I said. "I really wanted—"

She put her finger to my lips and smiled. "It's OK, sweetie. It really is."

I didn't know what else to say. But in that moment, calm overtook me, the way you feel when you're at the beach and a breeze glides in and your muscle tension releases, and everything just goes.

"Can we be friends?" I asked. "I know that's like the worst breakup line ever, but I don't want us to break up and act like nothing ever happened. I mean, I really, sincerely, honestly want to be your friend, and for you to be mine."

She laughed, not in a way that was at my expense, but rather endearing.

"You really are one in a million, Linus," she said, and I smiled. "We can try." After a beat, she asked, "Do you think your friend Jennifer and her husband will make it?"

"I really hope so."

"Maybe I'll reach out to her. I'll bet we have a lot in common."

"I think she'd really like that."

Sari kissed me on the cheek. "Take good care, Linus. I'll see you around." And with that, she left the gym.

Have you ever gotten that feeling as if everything that's happened in your entire life has led you to a singular moment, and you don't have a single regret because you wouldn't want to be anywhere else but there? When it's so crystal clear and you just *know*?

Yeah. That moment. That's when I found Jo-Jo, who had just thanked some patrons.

Jo-Jo was my intention made manifest. Not at midnight on New Year's Eve. Not that night at Angry Hank's. *Now.*

It wasn't even about Jo-Jo. It was about *me.*

Whatever happened, I was OK. Single or married, teaching or building, getting it right or making mistakes, I mattered.

And I knew exactly what I wanted to do.

NOW, REALLY, BACK TO NEW YEAR'S EVE ...

As midnight neared, Jo-Jo and I slow-danced to Ella Fitzgerald in the middle of Jenn and Larry's living room, right next to Sari and her new boyfriend, Derek. The universe has a sense of humor *and* a sense of romance.

"How are we going to top this year?" Jo-Jo asked.

"We can't," I said. "Let's just eat Pop-Tarts and watch old movies for all of 2018."

"Pop Tarts?"

"Naked," I added.

"Sold."

After the song ended, the countdown began. Everybody stopped what they were doing, stood in place, and chanted in unison.

Ten.

Nine.

Eight.

It was almost time.

"Actually, I've got a better idea," I said.

I reached into my pocket and withdrew the box.

Jo-Jo

In the end, everything begins again

I MUST HAVE BEEN THE LAST PERSON IN THE ROOM TO REALIZE WHAT LINUS was doing. Honestly, I thought maybe his knee had gone out on him—he had tweaked it a bit on my elliptical earlier in the week, and thus we decided he was getting plenty of exercise on the job.

But in an instant, I knew, and the murmur around us—the collective gasp in chorus—confirmed it.

My first reaction—panic. My life flashed before me—first, the no-good boyfriends, then the good-guys-but-emotionally-aloof-boyfriends, then Larry, then the conveyor belt of unmemorable one-off dates, then Rex ...

Seven.

Six.

Five.

Four.

Every single one of them was a mirror, revealing all the ways I'd first believed myself unworthy, then aloof, and then afraid, and then indifferent, and then willing to settle. My panic subsided when I realized Linus was just as much a mirror as the rest of them. He was the real deal because I'd finally stopped believing in a world that was against me. He showed me what kindness looked like because I'd finally allowed myself to see it. He was my friend because I'd finally stopped looking for a scapegoat.

Three.

Two.

He opened the ring box and turned it toward me. Yogo sapphire set in a simple platinum band. I'd said something offhanded about Yogos, what, six months ago, just how I liked that there was a Montana gemstone. He remembered. Of course he did.

I spoke to him through prayerful hands held over my mouth and nose. "You are incredible," I said.

"I really kind of am," he said.

And then softly, sweetly, he stood in place and spoke into my ear. "Will you marry me?"

"Only if you'll marry me," I replied. We were partners, after all.

One.

WE WENT HOME IN LINUS'S TRUCK, quiet, fingers laced together between the bucket seats. I knew Linus was the one that night in his kitchen, as he explained the crooked wall to me. Not in the soulmate, there's-one-person-for-each-person sort of way. Believe it or not, I don't buy the soulmate thing. I don't buy destiny. In a different circumstance, I could have ended up with Rex. Or even Larry. Or someone else.

But I ended up with Linus, and he with me. And that has made all the difference.

Everybody clapped and cheered and whistled for us, and for

2018, and that was awfully nice of them, but when Linus leaned into me after the hoopla died down and said "Want to go home?", that was when the rush of it all hit me.

Because home isn't just a town or a house or a lot on the city grid.

It's a commitment and a life together, and we started that long before I said yes to Linus's marriage proposal.

I TURNED DOWN THE LINENS. Toby took his place beside Linus's pillow. Cholly girl stretched herself out across the foot of the bed. Linus climbed in.

"Coming?" he asked.

"In a second. I just want to check on something."

I padded down the hallway into the living room. The streetlights cast sideways beams through the big front window. I opened the door and stepped onto the porch.

There, across the park, I saw my old house. So many people and events and images I thought would always be calcified in me, immovable. And it's all changed. Not that it didn't happen, but that it happened and it's part of the story, and the story goes on.

I looked up, beyond the line of trees, beyond the low-hanging clouds, deep into the frosty night. I stared, transfixed, and then, in the next instant, it was as if a voice told me that it was time for bed. To leave my ponderings for another day.

I went in. I locked the door. I found my way back to the bedroom. Linus had turned off the light and was already cutting snores. (No relationship is perfect, OK?) I slid under the sheet and comforter and nestled into him, and he opened his arms and gathered me in. He kissed my ear and whispered, "We're getting married."

"Yes," I said. "Yes, we are."

Mr. Blue Sky

This is forever, here within our hands

HOW DID JO-JO AND LINUS GET TOGETHER?

How does anyone get together?

It happened when they stopped wanting so much. When they let go of the need for more and made peace with what they had and where they were. A week after the gym opened, it wasn't any big deal for them to go to a movie together, to hold hands, to eat dinner afterward and talk right through it. When he drove her home, he walked her to the door, took her in his arms, and said, "Here's another one." And he kissed her again.

He didn't have to wonder if she'd let him. And she didn't have to wonder if he would call the next day.

They weren't doing or trying. They were simply being.

They had built their trust, so nothing seemed frantic or out of control. Their first sleepover—Linus's house, with Toby in the bed, next to his pillow—happened neither too soon nor too late.

The next morning, Toby nuzzled up to Jo-Jo as if she belonged, because she did. The next night, it was Linus and Jo-Jo and Cholly in her bed; the dog was a little possessive of Jo-Jo at first, having adopted much of the same behavior as her mama. But Jo-Jo (and here I must confess that I offered some backup support) assured her that Linus was not Rex, or any other man who had let her down. In fact, by now Jo-Jo didn't even see it as having been let down as much as having been released for better things. Where she was once resentful, she was now grateful.

I'm so proud of her. I'm proud of them both.

Jo-Jo told him she loved him over fettuccini and brick oven pizza at Ciao Mambo. He told her he loved her while backing out of a parking space at the paint store. (OK, so he doesn't exactly have the romantic thing down cold. Maybe we could get him to watch some Robert Redford movies.)

In short, it happened little by little. And then it seemed to happen all at once.

You might be thinking my work is now done where Jo-Jo and Linus are concerned. A self-important angel might even take a bow. But no. Everything that has happened in their lives has led to this moment. They figured out their home truths and learned their lessons. Things got worse before they got better. And now they're leading by example. But I'll stick around. It's a short story for you, but a long continuum for me. We've talked about this before.

As for Larry and Jennifer—they're not where they want to be yet, but every day, they're choosing to keep moving forward, together. Neither one is working at it as much as they are maintaining now. And it's daily maintenance. Someone once said "Love is a decision," but I disagree. Love is a constant. Acceptance and allowing are the decisions. I have faith in them, too, because they start every day at love. Who can do better than that?

These lives will continue to ebb and flow—Jo-Jo, Linus, Larry, Jennifer, Sari, Caroline, Cholly, Toby—all of them. And they'll touch other lives, and other lives will touch theirs. That's the way it works. And I'll continue to be present to it all, taking the journey, rooting for them—and you—every step of the way. How could I not? You—the collective you—gave the world Tony Randall and Jack Klugman in a horse costume on *Let's Make a Deal*. You're worth it.

I leave you with this: You are not human beings having a spiritual experience; you are spiritual beings having a human experience. It's a magnificent gift to take a turn on this mortal coil together. You truly can't take in the capacity of the awesomeness. Yes, there's a lot of senseless violence and disease and pollution and bad things happening to good people. There's crap TV and movies with way too much CGI. But there's also tremendous accomplishment that ripples farther and wider than any of that bad stuff. Mount Rushmore, for example. The polio vaccine. Multitrack audio recording. Earth, Wind, and Fire (the band, I mean, although the elements are cool, too). A Pakistani teenager who survived a gunshot to the head because she was a girl who wanted to go to school and ended up becoming an ambassador for peace.

Be the ripple.

The End
(and, of course, The Beginning)

Acknowledgments

COLLABORATING ON A NOVEL CAN BE FUN AND CHALLENGING. It can also be risky and a little scary when the collaborators are married. Fortunately, we found that we make a good team as writing partners, and we had a blast writing this story.

We'd like to thank the following for their support in birthing this book:

Our literary agent, Nalini Akolekar, who went to bat for us and for our story.

Our friends and colleagues Kelly Hewins, Karen McQuestion, Karen Booth, and Molly Duncan Campbell, for reading the novel in its early inceptions and offering kind words.

Helen Boyce, Tracy Fenton and the rest of the TBC gang on Facebook for always supporting us and sharing their passion for reading with others.

The Undeletables.

Our Billings friends, whom we love and miss and look forward to seeing soon.

This House of Books in Billings, Montana; Elk River Books in Livingston, Montana; and independent bookstores everywhere.

Our new community in midcoast Maine. We couldn't have chosen a better place to live.

Our Lorello, Lancaster, and Clines families. We love you.

Our readers who have supported our work for almost ten years. You make doing what we do worthwhile.

Spatz the cat.

—Elisa Lorello and Craig Lancaster
November 2018

About the authors

Photo by Casey Page

ELISA LORELLO IS A LONG ISLAND NATIVE, where she grew up with five brothers and a sister. She earned her bachelor's and master's degrees at the University of Massachusetts Dartmouth and taught rhetoric and writing at the college level for more than ten years.

She is the author of eleven novels, including the bestselling *Faking It*; a memoir; and a book about writing. She has been featured in *Montana Quarterly* and *Rachael Ray Every Day* magazines, and in Jane Friedman's blog series *5 On*. She continues to speak and write about her publishing experiences and to teach the craft of writing and revision.

Photo by Casey Page

CRAIG LANCASTER IS THE AUTHOR OF NINE BOOKS OF FICTION, including the bestselling series of novels featuring the character Edward Stanton (*600 Hours of Edward, Edward Adrift, Edward Unspooled*) as well as a collection of short stories. He is also a frequent contributor to magazines and newspapers as both a writer and an editor.

His work has been recognized by the Montana Book Awards, the High Plains Book Awards, the Utah Book Awards, the Independent Publisher Book Awards and others.

He grew up in North Texas. Before writing fiction, he worked at newspapers big and small in Texas, Alaska, Kentucky, Ohio, California, Washington, and Montana.

Connect with Elisa Lorello and Craig Lancaster

Elisa on the Web: www.elisalorello.com
Elisa on Twitter: @elisalorello
Elisa on Facebook: https://www.facebook.com/Elisa-Lorello-Author/

Craig on the Web: www.craig-lancaster.com
Craig on Twitter: @authorlancaster
Craig on Facebook: https://www.facebook.com/authorcraiglancaster/

Also by Elisa Lorello

Also by Craig Lancaster

  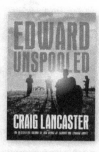 

CPSIA information can be obtained
at www.ICGtesting.com
Printed in the USA
BVHW040725041022
648592BV00001B/37

9 780997 643336